The House With Chicken Legs

'So good
you'll CLUCK with laughter!'
Pamela Butchart, author of
Baby Aliens Got My Teacher!

'Wonderfully **heart-warming**
and **absolutely hilarious**'
Catherine Doyle, author of
The Storm Keeper's Island

'Will have readers
snorting with giggles'
Northern Echo

'A **gloriously fun**, madcap
adventure with a **celebration
of friendship** at its heart.'
Anna James, author of *Pages & Co:
Tilly and the Bookwanderers*

'Hysterically funny!'

Books by Sam Copeland

PUFFIN BOOKS

Sam Copeland is an author, which has come as something of a shock to him. He is from Manchester and now lives in London with two smelly cats, three smelly children and one relatively clean-smelling wife. Sam also works as a dinosaur de-boner, removing skeletons from dinosaurs and giving them to museums. Once the museums have finished with them, he then re-bones the dinosaurs, much to their relief. *Charlie Turns Into a T-Rex* is his second book. Despite legal threats, he refuses to stop writing.

Follow Sam online:
www.sam-copeland.com
@stubbleagent
#CharlieTurnsIntoaTRex

SAM COPELAND

CHARLIE

ILLUSTRATED BY
SARAH HORNE.

TURNS INTO A

T-REX

PUFFIN

PENGUIN BOOKS

UK | USA | Canada | Ireland | Australia
India | New Zealand | South Africa

Penguin Books is part of the Penguin Random House group of companies
whose addresses can be found at global.penguinrandomhouse.com.

www.penguin.co.uk
www.puffin.co.uk
www.ladybird.co.uk

Penguin
Random House
UK

First published 2019

001

Text design by Janene Spencer
Printed in Great Britain by Clays Ltd, Elcograf S.p.A.

A CIP catalogue record for this book is available from the British Library

ISBN: 978–0–241–34622–8

All correspondence to
Penguin Books
Penguin Random House Children's
80 Strand, London WC2R 0RL

To my wife Lynne, for endlessly putting up with me.
To my children, Caoimhe, Conor and Sadie,
for making me endlessly put up with you.

Puffin Books

80 Strand

London

Dear Reader,

You might recall at the end of the previous 'book', *Charlie Changes Into a Chicken*, we recommended that you never read anything by the so-called author Sam Copeland ever again. We warned you that he was a disreputable liar and a writer of little talent.

And yet here we are.

Despite our stern warning, you have his new book in your hand. You have even begun to read it. Don't try to deny it. You're reading this sentence.

And this one.

Why aren't you stopping?

STOP READING NOW.

You're still reading, aren't you?

Why would you ignore such a clear warning? Perhaps you are the type of person that sticks their hand into a flame to see if it really is hot, or picks up a rabbit dropping and pops it in your mouth and starts chewing because you think it looks like a raisin, even though you've JUST been told, 'Don't put that in your mouth; it's a rabbit poo.' That might explain your actions.

Well, let us once again try to be as clear as possible: this next 'book' really is no better than the first. If anything, it's worse. Much worse. But then, as we have seen, you obviously don't listen to warnings.

You may also recall that we promised that we would never publish a book by Sam Copeland again. Unfortunately it has been brought to our attention by a large number of lawyers that we are legally obliged to publish this. That means by law we HAVE to. You didn't HAVE to read this book. You chose to. You have no such excuse.

If by some chance you are in a bookshop or library holding this book, simply put it down and walk away. We urge you to choose something more wholesome and educational instead.

And if it is too late, and you are sitting at home, perhaps curled in front of a crackling fire or cuddled up snug in bed, and have just settled down to reading this book, we have one thing to say:

We hope you hate reading this book as much as we hated publishing it.

Yours faithfully,
The Publisher

CHAPTER 1

Charlie McGuffin was being followed.

A malevolent shadow was watching him. Waiting.

Something – or someone – was stalking him through the corridors of the school. A dark presence, menacing, unseen and unknowable –

'Look, Dylan, I know it's you following me. I can see you there,' Charlie said, hands on hips. 'Can you actually stop? You just look weird doing it. Seriously, Dylan – come out from behind the pillar.'

Dylan stepped out from behind a pillar.

'And take that ridiculous hat off,' Charlie added.

1

Dylan took off the ridiculous hat, a floppy summer hat borrowed from his mum.

'And the sunglasses. Take those off as well.'

Dylan took off the sunglasses.

'Now *please* stop following me.'

Dylan stepped forward, chest puffed. 'You know you can run, McGuffin, but you can't hide. You. Can't. Hide.' A smile slid across Dylan's face like a slug trail. 'I'm your shadow. Your dark half. Wherever you go, I will be there. Hunting you. Ready to pounce like a . . . like a . . . frog.'

'A frog? A pouncing frog? Frogs don't even pounce.'

'Yes, they do. They pounce on flies. And you're my fly. Trapped in my web.'

'A . . . frog web?' said Charlie, looking a little baffled.

'You think you're so clever, McGuffin, don't you? Well, you're not. Your silly little friends might think you're a genius –'

'I'm not sure they do actually. In fact, I'm pretty certain Flora thinks I'm the total opposite. She even said that to me yesterday. She said "Charlie, you are actually the total opposite of a genius."'

'Enough!' Dylan held his hand up. 'Just know that I am going to capture you.' Dylan opened his hand. Inside was a matchbox. He shook it. It was empty. 'I am going to wait until you change into an animal. And I'm going to trap you. And then you won't be laughing. Or if you are, no one will hear you. Because you'll be trapped in a matchbox. A matchbox prison!'

Dylan started laughing to himself and then walked off, still laughing wildly, leaving Charlie standing alone in an empty corridor.

Charlie couldn't help it – Dylan was getting to him. He could feel his stress levels begin to rise, little shivers of electricity darting through him. This was the first sign that Charlie was about to change. He closed his eyes and breathed deeply a couple of times, focusing on his breathing. Then he opened his eyes wide.

'Hey, Dylan!' Charlie shouted to the small figure at the end of the long corridor. 'Dylan! I think I'm changing! Quick!'

Dylan turned round and began running back as fast as he could.

'Quick, Dylan! It's happening!'

Dylan sprinted as fast as he could. He reached Charlie, panting.

'Oh, sorry,' Charlie said. 'False alarm.'

Dylan glared at Charlie. 'WHAT?'

'I'm sorry!' Charlie said, grinning. 'I could have sworn I started feeling it. Ah, well, it's an unpredictable science, this whole changing business. Better luck next time. Actually there won't be a next time. You're wasting your time. I've worked out how to control it, you see, so I can absolutely guarantee a hundred per cent that there'll be no more Charlie changing into *anything*.'

Charlie winked at Dylan, and then walked off, laughing maniacally, leaving Dylan standing alone in the empty corridor.

AUTHOR'S NOTE

If you haven't read Book 1 in this series, *Charlie Changes Into a Chicken*, then you're probably pretty confused about what's going on right now.

Tough luck.

You should have bought Book 1.

You come waltzing in here thinking, *Oh, I don't need to read Book 1. I'm very clever and I'm sure I'll work out what's happening as I go along.*

Well, NOW who looks silly? You haven't a clue what's going on, have you? You don't know who Charlie is or who Dylan is or why Dylan is trying to put Charlie in a matchbox. All I can say is good luck with the rest of the book, dunderhead.

AUTHOR'S NOTE II

The publishers have informed me that apparently I am not allowed to refer to my 'valued readers' as 'dunderheads'. They have therefore instructed me to apologize to you. So, here we are:

I'm really, really, truly sorry.[1]

I hope you're happy.[2]

They have also instructed me to give you a quick run-down on what happens in Book 1. So, for those of you too lazy to go to the library to get it, here we go:

Charlie McGuffin keeps turning into animals. He discovers, with the help of his friends Flora, Mohsen and Wogan, that he changes when he is stressed and upset. Together

---

[1] I'm not really sorry. I lied. Dunderhead.

[2] I don't.

they work out that he can control it (sort of) if he relaxes and tries to be happy. Also, Charlie's nemesis, Dylan, who you just met, saw Charlie change and basically went very weird and turned into a bit of a movie villain who's determined to expose Charlie's secret to the whole world.

OK, now you've caught up, shall we get on with the story? Good.

CHAPTER 1
(CONTINUED)

'**W**ow! So you're sure you have the whole changing-into-an-animal thing under control?' asked Mohsen.

'Oh yes. Absolutely,' replied Charlie.

It was playtime, but he was sitting with Flora and Mohsen in a noisy classroom, as cold sleety rain was pattering against the window. Flora was absent-mindedly flicking through a magazine called *The World's Fluffiest But Deadly Animals*. The autumn term was coming to an end, and Christmas was on everybody's mind.

The class had spent the morning making paper chains, and they were now hung all across the classroom.

Wogan was over the other side of the room, talking to the new girl, Daisy. Daisy had long brown curly hair and she loved unicorns more than anything. And ponies. But mostly unicorns. Wogan had spent the whole of the past couple of days telling anybody who listened that he absolutely did *not* think Daisy was pretty and that he had, in fact, actually *always* thought unicorns were 'cool'.

'You're totally sure?' Flora said to Charlie, eyeing him suspiciously.

'Yes! Definitely. Sheesh! I told you. Dylan tried getting me to change in the corridor just now, but I stopped it. So I'm completely one hundred per cent sure that I am totally in control of the whole changing-into-an-animal thing and it won't happen again. I can guarantee that.'

Charlie couldn't guarantee that.

In fact, Charlie, deep down, wasn't at all sure that he had control of the whole changing-into-an-animal thing. But he wanted to be brave in front of Flora, who had managed to increase in awesomeness by about six per cent since Book 1 after winning the Interschool County Rap Battle with her rap 'Top Flor'.

'Charlie, you don't have to be brave in front of me, you know. You can tell me the truth,' Flora said, placing a hand on Charlie's shoulder.

'Will you stop putting that thing on me?' Charlie said, knocking the fake toy hand off his shoulder. 'Honestly, it's just weird.'

'Well, it's just . . . It's just . . . It's a big thing to have to learn and it might take time to get the hang of it completely,' said Flora, picking up her

toy hand and putting it in her bag. 'Don't be disappointed if you do change again.'

Charlie made a humphing noise.

Mohsen wandered over. 'Hey, Charlie,' he said. 'Have you changed into any animals again?'

'NO! I HAVE NOT! I CAN CONTROL IT, OK?' Charlie snapped.

Mohsen and Wogan edged away from Charlie.

'O-K,' said Mohsen, holding his hands up. 'That's great. Good for you.'

'Guys!' whispered Flora. 'Keep it down! We don't want everyone to hear!'

'It really is quite amazing,' said Mohsen in a low voice, 'that you, a small boy of just nine years of age, have succeeded so easily in totally mastering your mysterious and extraordinary power, the likes of which mankind has never seen before.'

Charlie narrowed his eyes. 'You don't believe me! You don't think I have mastered it! Well, I have. It won't happen again,' said Charlie certainly.

★★★

Well, thought Charlie later that very evening, as he began licking himself clean, *I was certainly wrong*.

And why was Charlie licking himself clean?

Well, to find that out let's go back a short while in time . . .

Charlie had arrived home feeling pretty chipper. It had been a good day: his class had had the supply teacher in all day, because their usual teacher, Arthur Wind, was on a three-day intensive strategy course with the headteacher, Miss Fyre, on a boat on the Norfolk Broads.

Mr Pointment, the supply teacher, had let them sit wherever they liked, *and* had let them do whatever they wanted in class as long as they were *very* quiet and hadn't bothered him. He had sat at the front of the class for almost the whole day, eyes closed and holding his head in his hands, apart from a couple of times when he'd suddenly run out of the room, a look of pale urgency on his face.

Charlie's good mood was spoilt not long after he got home. He and SmoothMove (Charlie's big brother who had been ill but was now much better) had wolfed down their tea and were lying in front of the TV under the glow of the Christmas-tree lights, playing *FIFA 19*.

Charlie was losing as per usual.

They heard the key in the front door. It was their dad, home unusually early. He didn't poke his head into the sitting-room to say hello, which was also unusual.

Charlie and SmoothMove could hear a low muttered conversation between their mum and dad coming from the kitchen. They could tell by the tone of their parents' voices that all wasn't right. SmoothMove and Charlie looked at each other.

'What's that all about?' asked Charlie.

'Dunno,' SmoothMove replied. 'Boring adult stuff, I reckon.' He shrugged, then turned back to the game, but a nervous tension still rippled between them.

A little while later, their mum called them both into the kitchen. They both wandered in. Their mum and dad were sat at the table, both looking serious, both with their arms crossed.

'Could you sit down?' Charlie's dad said. 'We

need to have a family conference.'

Charlie knew a family conference meant something big. Either something good-big or something bad-big. Unless Charlie was very much mistaken, the looks on his parents' faces said this was something bad-big. His first thought was something was wrong with SmoothMove again, but his brother was sitting opposite him looking healthy and equally mystified at his dad's behaviour, so it couldn't be *that*.

'I'm afraid to say,' his dad announced, 'we're going to have to tighten our belts a little for a while.'

'Why? Are we losing weight?' Charlie asked.

'No, Charlie. It's an expression. It means we are going to have to save some money. A lot of money actually.'

This sounded like pretty terrible news to Charlie, especially as Christmas was fast approaching.

'You see,' continued his dad. 'There's been a bit of trouble at work and it could have some pretty serious repercussions.'

Charlie thought that Reaper Cushions sounded both awesome and comfortable but knew, by looking at his dad's face, that now was not the time to say that.

'What sort of repercussions, Dad?' SmoothMove asked.

'Well, it looks like we might have to downsize.'

'Downsize? How do you mean?' Charlie asked.

'I mean that we might have to sell the house,' his father replied.

Silence hit the kitchen. Charlie stared at his dad.

'And then what?' asked SmoothMove. 'Where will we live?'

'Well, there's a chance we might have to move in with Aunt Brenda. Just for a short while. Until we sort things out more permanently.'

'Aunt Brenda?!' cried Charlie. 'We can't move in with Aunt Brenda!'

Aunt Brenda's house was all the way over the other side of town and it smelled of cat wee.

hi KIDDIES!

BRRRR...

Aunt Brenda had seventeen cats and one leg. She refused to get a fancy modern prosthetic leg, and as she walked around her house her wooden leg rapped on the floorboards like the deck of a pirate ship.

'Now, it's not certain,' his dad continued. 'Nothing's set in stone. Fingers crossed, we'll be able to sort out the work issue and everything will just go back to normal. But in the meantime we're going to have to make a few savings.' Charlie's dad gave the table a watery smile.

'But try not to worry, kids. We'll all pull together as a family,' said Charlie's mum. 'And if the worst comes to the worst, we can sell one of you,' she continued with a twinkle in her eye.

'Oh, that's a good idea!' said Dad, a cheeky smile crinkling his face. 'That would be a proper money-saver. But it will be too tough to decide which one of you to keep, so you boys need to do rock-paper-scissors and the loser gets eBayed.'

They all laughed, breaking the tension a little.

But although his dad might have been smiling again, Charlie couldn't mistake the shadow of concern still clouding his father's eyes. And that shadow gave Charlie a knot in his stomach.

CHAPTER 2

After a meal full of forced laughter, Charlie trudged upstairs, the knot in his stomach twisting tighter. He flopped on to his bed, staring at the ceiling, hands by his side. What exactly had happened at his dad's work? Why was it so serious?

If Charlie was completely honest, he wasn't even sure what his dad's work involved. Something to do with computers? Inventing stuff, maybe? Charlie had asked umpteen times before, but whenever his dad had started replying with 'Well, son, I mean, I have explained this to you a number of times before, but never mind, my job involves . . .' he just switched off. He couldn't help it. His ears stopped working. And now something was happening at his dad's work that could mean they might have to sell their house and move in with Aunt Brenda?! Charlie groaned.

A feeling, and yet not a feeling – a memory of a feeling – rippled through his body unnoticed.

Would he have to share a room with SmoothMove?

Charlie was so preoccupied with worrying, he didn't even notice his fingers beginning to crackle with static or his right eye twitching.

I mean, SmoothMove smelled *awful*. He never changed his socks. Charlie couldn't possibly share a room with him – he'd have to wear one of those gas masks he'd seen in history lessons about the First World War.

His left eye twitching. Both eyes twitching.

And what happened if they couldn't stay with Aunt Brenda? What if they had to move areas? What if Charlie had to start a new school? Rumour had it that Huntsman's School for Boys – the only other school in town, which was located in a converted Victorian prison – made their students play full-contact rugby. In their underpants. In winter.

By the time Charlie recognized the electricity searing through his body, it was too late.

I'm changing! Charlie thought in total panic. *No! I've got it under control!*

He quickly started slowing his breathing down, trying to calm himself, but he could already feel the squeezing feeling, like he was being shot down a wire into a plug socket.

Think happy thoughts! Think happy thoughts! Charlie tried telling himself, remembering that it was being happy that had stopped him from changing in front of the whole school during the school play. But the only thoughts his brain would allow him to think were of moving schools and SmoothMove's crusty socks.

Charlie could feel fur springing out of his skin, millions of short hairs covering his arms, his face, his body.

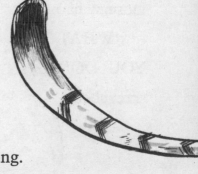

And now, he was shrinking.

His teeth like tiny daggers.

Fingernails into claws.

A tail.

It was too late.

Charlie had changed.

Now, Charlie had a fair idea what he had turned into, but it was confirmed when Chairman Meow wandered into his bedroom. Chairman Meow was the family ginger cat and was usually pretty chill, apart from the time he had tried to eat Charlie when Charlie was a spider. But we all make mistakes.

However, the moment Chairman Meow clapped eyes on Charlie this time, all hell broke loose.

'WHAT THE – WHO THE – WHAT ARE YOU DOING IN HERE?!' Chairman Meow screeched.

Charlie could understand him – and that meant one thing: Charlie was a cat.

'A CAT! THERE'S A CAT IN HERE! I HATE CATS!' Chairman Meow screamed.

He had puffed up to about ten times his normal size, his tail huge and fluffy. He was arching his back, standing on his tippy-claws, trying to make himself as big as possible.

'GET OUT OF HERE, UNKNOWN INTRUDER CAT, OR I WILL DESTROY YOU! I WILL SHRED YOU TO TINY PIECES! BUT FIRST, AS IS TRADITION BEFORE CAT-WAR, I MUST SING THE CAT-SONG OF DEATH!'

And with that Chairman Meow began howling.

'Can you PLEASE stop screeching like that? Goodness me, *what* a racket,' Charlie meowed.

Chairman Meow glared at Charlie. 'Answer me, unknown intruder cat. Who are you? Tell me your name before I resume the Cat-Song of Death.'

'I'm –'

'One moment! There is dirt on me!' Chairman Meow began licking one leg furiously. 'There. I am clean. You may continue.'

'I'm Charlie! Your owner!' Charlie said quickly.

'My WHAT? You are very much mistaken, strange-smelling intruder cat. I have no owner.'

'You do! Your name is Chairman Meow, and you belong to the McGuffin family.'

'My name is Chairman Meow?! Once again you are very much mistaken, foolish stranger cat. My name is Deathclaw Litterborn of the House Felis, the First of His Name, the Untamed, King of the Canis and the First Cats, Cateesi of the Great Grass Garden, Eater of Birds and Father of Kittens.'

Charlie blinked at Chairman Meow. 'I . . . I beg your pardon?' he ventured.

'I said my name is Deathclaw Litterborn of the House –'

'No! Please. Stop. I heard you the first time. I'm just surprised. We've been getting your name wrong all these years.'

'I am certain you have. Now, you dim-witted kitty, I have told you who I am. Who are *you*?

Quickly now. I haven't cleaned myself properly in over thirty minutes.'

'I've told you who I am! I'm –'

'Stop! A moment!' Chairman Meow began licking his back. 'There. I am clean. You were saying?'

Watching Chairman Meow clean himself, Charlie couldn't help feeling that there must be some dirt on one of his own paws that urgently needed licking off . . .

'I was saying I'm Charlie!' Charlie said, trying to stop himself from licking his paw. 'You know me – you sleep on my bed every night!'

Chairman Meow stared at Charlie, his eyes narrowing in recognition. 'You are the Small Idiot Human?'

'What do you mean "Small Idiot Human"?'

'Every night I sleep on the bed of the Small Idiot Human. Are you the Small Idiot Human?'

'Well, yes. But hang on – I'm not –'

'You are the spawn of the Large Female Idiot Human and the Large Male Idiot Human.'

'You know, I'm starting to think you've got a real attitude problem,' said Charlie.

'I am uncertain whether you are male or female,' Chairman Meow continued.

'What do you mean you don't know if I'm male or female? I'm a boy!'

'It is difficult to tell. Especially because I can't bear looking at your ugly face.'

'My WHAT?' hissed Charlie indignantly, licking his paw clean.

'Although sometimes I just stare at you and am stunned at how ugly you are. And those times when I can bear to look at you, I see neither male nor female,' Chairman Meow continued, oblivious to Charlie's indignation. 'The other idiot human child smells more repulsive than you so I assumed perhaps he was an idiot human boy and you might be an idiot human girl.'

Charlie couldn't help but see some logic in that.

'Well, if I'm so repulsive, how come you sit on my knee all the time?'

'Stupid creatures are just as warm as clever ones. Anyway, I tire of you. I must leave this room and find another room with a closed door for me to scratch at, for reasons that you cannot comprehend. And then I must hit the other cat on the head, for other reasons that your tiny mind cannot begin to comprehend.'

'The other cat! You mean The Great Catsby?' Charlie said, licking one of his other paws and cleaning his face.

Chairman Meow looked at Charlie blankly.

'Oh! You probably don't call her The Great Catsby!' Charlie continued. 'You probably call her something like Daggerteeth Catclaws, Slayer of Mice, Sitter in Boxes –'

'The cat that sits in boxes?' Chairman Meow replied. 'No. That cat is called Miss Fluffikins.'

'Miss Fluffikins? How come she gets –'

'Do not ask. You should know by now that your tiny mind could not possibly comprehend the mind of a cat. Now, I must leave. To nap and try to forget your tiresome idiotic presence.' Chairman Meow started walking to the door, but turned back to Charlie. 'I do have one question for you.'

'What? Anything as long as you don't call me idiot again.'

'Every day I lay my special brown cat-eggs in –'

'Brown cat-eggs? Do you mean your poo?'

'Do not interrupt. Every day I lay my special brown cat-eggs in the tray of gravel. And every day an idiot human steals them. Why? What do you do with them, brown-cat-egg-stealing idiot humans?'

'We don't STEAL your poo, we –'

'Yes you do. I watch you. You scrape it up and put it in a bag – for what sick and twisted reason I cannot even begin to imagine. You really are foul, ugly, idiotic creatures.'

And with that Chairman Meow flounced out of the room, nose in the air, tail erect.

Charlie was alone. And was a cat. And he now had a new-found dislike of cats. He began absent-mindedly licking himself clean, thinking about how Flora had been right about him changing again, and how she was *always* right about *everything*, when three things happened in a row:

1. Charlie heard the muttering voices of his parents from downstairs, and realized if he could hear what they were saying it might give him more of an idea of what was going on.

2. Charlie started licking his bum clean.

3. Charlie remembered that he really shouldn't be licking his bum clean, and started spitting and coughing and retching.

When he had finished wanting to be sick all over his bedroom floor, he steeled himself, and padded silently out of his room, down the stairs and up to the kitchen door so he could hear his mum and dad talking more clearly.

'But surely they can't get away with it!' Charlie heard his mum say.

'They can. And they will. We're in real trouble,' Charlie's dad replied. 'It means we've lost exclusivity on the whole project. And they're much bigger than us – they can afford to sell it much cheaper than we can, which means we're in big, big trouble.'

'But can't you prove it's yours? You've worked on it for years. They can't just steal it from you!'

What!? Charlie thought. *Has someone stolen one of Dad's inventions?*

'You know what Van der Gruyne Industries are like. They've got armies of lawyers. The minute I try anything they will crush us with lawsuits. We can't afford that.'

Van der Gruyne Industries? That was Dylan's dad's company! What had they done?

'It's corporate espionage!' his mum cried. 'It's illegal!'

'We can't prove it,' his dad replied glumly. 'And they have it now. It's too late. And if we're not careful, they'll swallow McGuffin & Sons whole.'

'So that's it?' his mum said, sounding desperate. 'We just give up? We don't even fight? That's our future they've stolen.'

There was a long silence before Charlie's father replied. 'We'll think of something.' He didn't sound in the least bit hopeful.

'And while we're thinking, we lose our house, our home?' Charlie's mum was clearly angry.

She suddenly opened the door, and caught Charlie red-pawed.

'What the . . .? There's a strange cat in the house!'

Charlie's mum walked to the front door, opened it and tried shooing Charlie out, but Charlie wasn't particularly keen to go outside, as it was raining. Charlie's mum disappeared into the kitchen and reappeared a moment later holding a laser pointer. She shone it centimetres from Charlie's nose.

The moment the red dot appeared, Charlie was transfixed. He just *had* to catch it.

Charlie tried resisting, he really did. But the way it moved – it was too tempting . . .

Must . . . try to . . . resist . . .

And before Charlie knew what was happening, he had chased the laser spot outside, and the front door was shut forcefully behind him.

Charlie sat on the doorstep, feeling pretty shamefaced. He pondered his situation. It was raining heavily, and Charlie wondered how he was going to get back into the house. And how long his family might even *have* a house.

A leaf, fluttering in the wind, caught his eye. It looked like a mouse. A *dangerous* mouse that needed *killing*. Charlie crouched, still and silent, and then, when the leaf was least expecting it, he pounced, grabbed the leaf in his mouth, began chewing it, rolling on the ground, and then –

Then Charlie began to change back.

Before he knew it, he was back to Charlie. Except he was Charlie with a leaf in his mouth.

He took it out, feeling slightly embarrassed.

Charlie dismissed his embarrassment until later – for now he needed to get back in the house. He considered his options. He quickly decided against shinning up the drainpipe as he had never shinned up anything in his life and wasn't convinced he even knew how to shin, so didn't fancy his chances. Besides, there weren't even any windows open. Vaulting over the fence to the back door would be pointless as that would be locked at this time of the evening. There was nothing else for it – Charlie had to ring the doorbell.

His mum opened the door, a look of shock on her face when she saw Charlie standing outside, dripping wet.

'What on earth are you doing out here, Charles McGuffin?!'

'I . . . er . . . I was just looking at the . . . moon . . . and the door shut behind me.'

Charlie knew he sounded pretty unconvincing.

'You can't even see the moon! It's pouring with rain. You're absolutely soaking wet. And is that a bit of leaf sticking out of your mouth? What have you been doing? Get inside, now!'

★★★

As Charlie climbed into bed that evening, questions whirled round his head. What had been stolen from his dad? What did Dylan's dad's company have to do with it? And why had he acted so strangely when he was a cat? It was all very worrying. He'd have to talk to his friends about it all in the morning.

He'd tried to eat a leaf, for goodness' sake. He'd even licked his own *bum* clean.

But there was no way he was telling Flora, Mohsen and Wogan *that*.

CHAPTER 3

'**S**o how exactly did you behave strangely?' asked Flora, looking sideways at Charlie.

Charlie was walking home with Flora, Mohsen and Wogan, and he'd told them everything that had happened the previous evening.

Nearly everything.

'Yeah, come on, Charlie,' said Mohsen. 'You can tell us anything.'

'That's right,' said Wogan. 'We are all really good secret-keepers here. I mean, everybody knows I never tell anybody *anything*. Like, remember the time you told me you were in love with Flor–'

'Wogan!' Charlie shouted.

Mohsen's jaw was on the floor. Flora was blushing furiously.

'Can we please just concentrate on what's important here?' Charlie continued, clearly panicking.

Flora stopped walking, and they all stopped with her. She looked hard at Charlie.

'Charlie, whatever happened, it would be much better for you to share it. We won't judge you.'

'OK,' said Charlie, taking a deep breath. 'I ate a leaf and licked my bum clean.'

For the second time in a matter of minutes, Mohsen's jaw hit the floor.

'You whatted your what-what?' Wogan asked Charlie, then turned to the others. 'What did he say he did? I *thought* I heard him say he licked his own bum clean! I mean, imagine! How disgusting would *that* be?'

'You heard right,' said Charlie, looking thoroughly miserable. 'That's what I mean. I *was* disgusting. And I've no idea why I did it.'

'Charlie, you have absolutely nothing to be ashamed of,' said Flora, eyes full of concern. 'We are all –'

'Did it taste horrible?' Wogan butted in. 'When you licked your bum? It must have done.'

Flora glared at Wogan. 'Wogan! Now is not the time.'

'That's right,' said Mohsen. 'We need to

focus. We can't do anything about what Charlie did. We should probably try to forget about it, although I'm not sure I'll ever be able to. Anyway, what we *can* do is start thinking about what to do about Charlie's dad and what Dylan's dad nicked off him.'

They all nodded in agreement.

'You're sure you've no idea what it was?' Mohsen continued.

'No. No idea at all,' Charlie replied, downcast.

'Well, that's the first thing we need to do: find out what exactly it is they've stolen.'

'What use will that be?' asked Charlie.

'Ah, well, I have a plan,' said Mohsen, waggling his eyebrows up and down. Flora, Charlie and Wogan stopped in their tracks and stared at Mohsen. 'And it's a plan so clever you could stick a fuzzy wig on it and call it Albert Einstein.'

'Whoa. Hang on. Stop right there,' Wogan said, holding his hand up. 'We all know that

Flora is the plan-maker in this group. I'm not sure I'm comfortable swapping roles like that. I mean, what next? Maybe I should swap with Charlie and then I could go around confessing my undying love for Flor–'

'Wogan!' shouted Charlie. 'Sheesh. I mean, come on.'

'We should hear Mohsen out,' said Flora. 'I want to hear the plan.'

'OK,' said Mohsen, looking around furtively to make sure nobody else was listening. 'Listen up. Here's what we do. We find out what Dylan's dad's company stole. Then we break in to their office and steal it back.'

'OK. Interesting,' said Flora. 'How do we do that?'

'How? Well, I dunno,' said Mohsen, shrugging. 'I hadn't got that far.'

'Yeah,' said Wogan. 'That's not really a plan then. That's more of an idea than a plan.'

'It is a plan!' said Mohsen, looking a little hurt.

'Whatever it is, why does everything always end up with me breaking in to somewhere?'[3] said Charlie. 'And Van der Gruyne Industries has serious security. It has massive high gates and guards. It has guard dogs. It has drones with laser-guided nuclear missiles.'

'Hang on,' said Flora. '*Drones with laser-guided nuclear missiles?* How exactly do you know they have those?'

'Erm . . . I think it was

[3] In Book 1, the internationally bestselling and stunningly reviewed *Charlie Changes Into a Chicken*, Charlie had to break in to his head teacher's office and shave a monkey. A toy monkey, not a real one.

actually Dylan who told me . . .'

'Yes, well, then I think we can probably forget the laser-guided nuclear drones, Charlie.'

'OK, thinking about it, we probably can. But high gates! Security guards! Dogs! They are all *very* real.'

'Hmm,' hmmed Flora. 'It won't be easy. It is a good plan, Mohsen –'

'A good *idea*,' said Wogan.

'It just needs a bit of *development*. I'll put my mind to it. But first, Charlie – you need to find out exactly what's been stolen . . .'

★★★

The opportunity to find out what exactly had been stolen came Charlie's way a few days later, and Charlie being Charlie he grabbed the opportunity with both hands and ran with it.[4]

---

[4] Unfortunately, Charlie being Charlie, he then tripped over and the opportunity went flying out of his hands high into the air before hitting the ground and smashing into tiny pieces . . .

The McGuffins had all gone into town to celebrate SmoothMove's birthday and, abandoning the new money-saving regime for the afternoon, were splashing out on a pizza-and-ice-cream family lunch. Despite the cold weather, they were sitting outside in the town square by the cathedral, happily lapping at their ice creams, watching Christmas shoppers rush by, laden with shopping bags.

The Christmas lights were on, and in the middle of the square, beside the huge Christmas tree, there was a real-life nativity scene with an actual real-live donkey. The donkey was eating the hay that was lining the baby Jesus's crib, and Joseph was straining at its lead trying to pull it away. SmoothMove and Mum were deep in conversation about who'd win a wrestling fight between four koala bears and the Queen.

It was the first time Charlie had been at least half alone with his dad since he'd agreed to find out what had been stolen. He had to grab the opportunity. He took a deep breath.

'Dad? Tell me again, what *exactly* is your job?'

Charlie was absolutely determined to listen and understand this time.

'Well, Charlie – I mean, I have explained this to you lots of times before – but I provide computer coding for IT and networking solutions.'

Nope, thought Charlie. *I still haven't a clue what that means.*

'Erm . . .'

'Essentially,' his dad continued, 'I invent computer programs that help other companies.'

Ah! thought Charlie. *I was right. My dad is an inventor!*

Charlie let that sink in for a few moments

while he plucked up the courage to ask what he *really* needed to know.

'Daaaad?' he said.

'Mmm-hmm?' his dad replied absent-mindedly, licking his ice cream, eyes closed, head lifted to the sunshine.

'Sooo . . . I overheard you and Mum talking the other day and you said that the reason our company is in trouble was something was stolen –'

His dad looked at him with a seriously serious look on his face. 'You know you *really* shouldn't be listening in to conversations that don't concern you, Charlie.'

'I know! It was an accident! Honestly. I promise. Sorry. But I was wondering . . . so . . . what *was* stolen?'

'Well, we think – but can't prove – that our main competitor took something very important from our company,' his father said.

'What? What was taken?' Charlie asked breathlessly.

It was the worst possible time for the cathedral bells to start ringing. But ring they did.

'Well, we think they stole some co–**BOOOONG**–de,' his dad said.

'Some *what*?' Charlie replied, straining to hear over the sound of the bells.

'I SAID THEY STOLE SOME CO–**BOOOONG**–DE!' his dad shouted over the deafening ringing.

'WHAT? THEY STOLE SOME GO–**BOOONG**–LD?'

'YES! THAT'S RIGHT! SOME CO–**BONG**–DE.'

'Wow! That's amazing!' Charlie said, his mind whirling. He wasn't sure why his dad would have gold in his office if he was just an inventor, but it made sense that someone would want to steal it.

'I didn't imagine you'd find it that exciting,' his dad said.

'You kidding? It's the most exciting thing I've heard in ages!'

Suddenly Charlie thought his dad was way cooler than he ever had done before.

Charlie's dad ruffled Charlie's hair. 'Don't tell your mum I told you, OK?' he said, then gave Charlie a wink.

Awesome! Charlie thought. *My dad is an inventor and had* gold *stolen.*

And Charlie was going to steal it back.

An hour or so later, the four of them were waiting for the bus to take them home. A cold light rain had started and it was dark, and the memory of the pizza and ice cream was slowly disappearing.

Headlights shone in the rain, and Charlie squinted to see if it was a bus. It wasn't. It was a long black car with tinted windows and it pulled in noiselessly into the bus stop.

A dark window slid down. Out of the window poked the perfectly groomed blond head of Mr Van der Gruyne. He looked horribly like an older Dylan.

'Treating your family to a ride on a bus, are you, McGuffin?' Mr Van der Gruyne said to Charlie's dad. 'How jolly.'

Charlie didn't like Mr Van de Gruyne's tone

one little bit. And he didn't like the look of pleasure in his pale blue eyes.

'Just drive on, Van der Gruyne,' Charlie's dad said gruffly.

'Sure I can't offer you a lift? You'd all fit in here no problem.'

'We don't want a lift from the likes of you,' said Charlie's mum, crossing her arms. 'I'd rather walk on broken glass.'

Charlie suddenly felt very proud of his parents standing up to Mr Van der Gruyne.

'Oh dear,' said Mr Van der Gruyne, licking his pink lips delicately. 'Looks like something has upset you all! Can't think *what* it could be. Well, must be getting on! Business is *so* busy for me at the moment. I'm sure you understand. Merry Christmas, McGuffin!'

The window slid back up and the car drove off, leaving the McGuffin family standing together in the rain.

'Ugh. That family is repulsive,' said Flora, shaking her head.

'Yeah, well, forget them! Let's focus on the big news – it was *gold* that was stolen!' Mohsen said, eyes wide. 'That is the most awesome thing I have ever heard.'

Charlie was reporting to his friends what had happened the day of SmoothMove's birthday and what he'd found out.

'Apart from when Charlie told us about the whole turning-into-animals malarkey. That was definitely more awesome,' Wogan said in a surprising turn of wisdom.

'That's true, Wogan. Fair point. But on a scale of awesomeness, Charlie's dad hiding a stash of gold scores pretty high.'

'Oh yes. Agreed,' Wogan said thoughtfully. 'But then it's also definitely not as awesome as that assembly when I sneezed and farted at the same time.'

Mohsen nodded. 'That *was* extremely awesome. We do seem to have a *lot* of awesomeness in our lives.'

Flora and Charlie stood open-mouthed at the ongoing conversation.

'Can we focus please, guys?' said Flora.

'Sorry! We just think it's awesome,' said Mohsen.

'We gathered,' said Flora.

'I never thought my dad had it in him,' Charlie said. 'Hiding gold and stuff. I wonder what else he's up to.'

'It is strange, though, isn't it? I mean why does your dad even have gold hidden?' asked Mohsen.

Wogan nodded. 'All my dad has hidden is his gnome collection in the cellar, which Mum won't let him have in the garden.'

'It doesn't seem particularly like him,' said

Flora. 'Are you sure you got it right, Charlie? Maybe you misheard him?'

'No!' Charlie exploded. 'I'm absolutely certain. He definitely said they stole some gold.'

As he spoke, Charlie remembered the loud clanging of the cathedral bells, and a tiny worm of nervous uncertainty reared its head. But just as quickly the bird of ignoring nagging doubt swooped down and gobbled the worm up in one. Before Charlie had time to think about it any more, an unwelcome interruption disturbed the four friends.

'Well, well, well,' said Dylan, as he approached with his best friend and fellow school bully Teddy. 'Look who it is. Nerds of a feather.'

Teddy laughed uncertainly at Dylan's joke, panicked confusion in his eyes.

'What do *you* want?' said Wogan, stepping forward towards Dylan.

'I just want to see how Charlie's doing. To see if he's feeling a bit *ruff*? Nothing *fishy* about that. And doesn't McGuffin speak for himself or is he too *chicken*?'

'Yeah, very funny, Dylan,' Charlie said. 'But if that's all you want, why don't you and your teddy bear just push off?'

Teddy growled at Charlie and took a menacing step towards him, but Dylan held him back.

'No need, Teddy,' Dylan said, grinning. 'So, Charlie? How's everything going with your dad?'

'What?' said Charlie, glaring at him.

'My dad said business was a bit tough for him at the moment.'

Charlie sprang forward and grabbed Dylan's collar. 'What do you know?'

Dylan shoved Charlie backwards. 'Ooh, looks like somebody's getting stressed,'

he gloated. 'I hope you don't start turning *wild* on me.'

'Just leave him, Charlie. He's trying to wind you up,' said Mohsen.

'That's an excellent suggestion, Mohsen. Let's go,' said Flora. She took Charlie's hand and led him away.

'Hey! Charlie!' Dylan shouted to the retreating friends.

Charlie turned round with a face like thunder. 'What?'

'I can't wait for you to get home and see what I saw them putting up in your garden this morning!'

Charlie had no idea what Dylan was talking about, and despite not wanting Dylan's words to get to him, he couldn't help but think about it for the rest of the day.

He saw it as soon as he turned into his road on the way home.

Right in the middle of the garden.

A for-sale sign.

CHAPTER 4

The moment Charlie saw the sign, stress and fear and anger hit him like a train. He felt like his stomach was falling out of his bum. A *for-sale* sign? So quickly? They were going to move? To *where*? To Aunt Brenda's and her stinky cats? His parents had said it would take ages! They'd *lied* to him. And now everybody would know they were having to move because they couldn't afford their house any more. Embarrassment and worry flooded his body.

His thoughts raced away. His heart began to pound.

And standing there, on the corner of his

street where anybody could see him, Charlie started to change.

He tried breathing slowly, imagining his happy place, but he was outside, and that heaped more stress on top of the first stress.

What if someone sees me?

He tried thinking of happy, funny memories, but all he could picture was the uncertain future stretching out in front of him. There was no stopping the change this time.

He had to get inside. He started running towards his house, but already he could feel the fire racing through him, every cell in his body being stretched and squeezed, bristly fur sprouting all over him. He couldn't ring the doorbell – his mum would drop dead of a heart attack if she opened the door to see her youngest son halfway into changing into a wombat or whatever it was he was turning into.

No – Charlie couldn't go home, and that meant he had to find somewhere to hide, and fast. He dropped his bag on the doorstep and started running back the way he'd come, his mind a whirl of panic.

He suddenly found it easier to run on all fours.

His hands were turning into huge paws.

His breath was coming out in snorts.

He was growing big – as big as one of the small cars he was running blindly past.

Charlie forced himself to stop, desperately trying to think sensibly. He took stock of his situation. He was standing in the middle of the street where he lived and he had turned into – what *had* he turned into? He was huge, with enormous paws and knife-like claws, and when Charlie looked down he saw he was covered in white fur. That could only mean one thing.

Charlie was a polar bear.

And being a polar bear in a quiet residential street was far from ideal – in fact, it was pretty un*bear*able.[5]

Great, thought Charlie. *Just great. I'm trying to hide but I can't because I'm an ENORMOUS polar bear. And Mum and Dad are selling our house. Things can't get* **any** *worse.*

---

[5] You will find this joke in *Guinness World Records 2019*, in the section 'World's Worst Jokes', subsection 'Jokes So Bad They Will Make You Want to Go and Live the Rest of Your Life in a Dark, Damp Cave'.

But as anybody who has been following Charlie's adventures will know, just when Charlie thinks things can only get better, they tend to get much worse.

And this time was no exception.

Just as Polar-Charlie started thumping down the street again, desperately looking for a hiding place, Mrs Shufflebottom (the elderly childminder with a cloud of snow-white hair, who lived next door to Charlie and always picked up a gaggle of Reception kids from Charlie's school) rounded the corner, a crocodile line of five small children skipping behind her.

They practically bumped into Charlie.

Now, I think we can all agree Charlie was having a bad day. He was worried about his dad and losing his home *and* he'd turned into a polar bear. Definitely a bad day.

However, that was a walk in the park on a sunny day eating chocolate ice cream with sprinkles compared to the day Mrs Shufflebottom and the children she was looking after were having.

They were walking down the street, minding their own business, when they turned the corner and were suddenly faced with a massive three-metre-tall 400-kilogram polar bear. Mrs Shufflebottom froze in terror, too scared to make a noise. The children, though, didn't have any such problem – they let out a scream so loud and so high it nearly burst Charlie's eardrums.

Polar-Charlie reared up on his hind legs and roared in fright.

This did not help matters – quite the opposite, in fact. From Mrs Shufflebottom and the children's perspective, a polar bear was now standing in front of them, rearing up to its full height and roaring at them at the top of its lungs.

By this point, three of the five children had, understandably, weed in their pants in terror. It would be impolite to discuss whether Mrs Shufflebottom had weed in her pants. Some things are best left to the imagination. Let's just say there were some bloomers in soak that evening.

Mrs Shufflebottom finally found her feet, turned round and started running the opposite direction from Charlie, arms flailing. She had quite forgotten about the children. One by one, the children recovered enough to start running away from Charlie as fast as they possibly could.

Charlie also decided running away as fast as he possibly could was the best course of action. So he did exactly that.

Little did he realize, though, that, as he ran back towards his house, Ava Braithwaite from Year Seven, who lived three doors down from Charlie, had also spotted him and, being rather braver than Mrs Shufflebottom (or at least standing at a safer distance), decided an Instagram

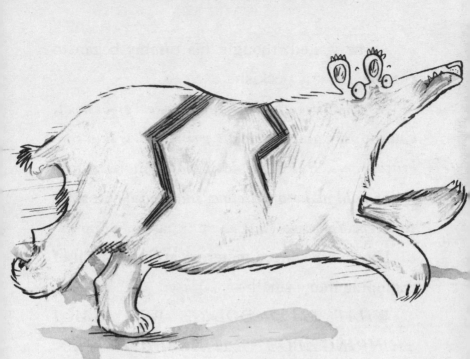

post of a polar bear was too good to miss. So she got her phone out and started filming Polar-Charlie pounding down the pavement.

Charlie ducked behind a tree, panting. He'd be safe here, completely hidden by the tree, until he started to change, at which point he could run into his garden and turn back to Charlie in privacy.

As he waited, though, his tummy began to rumble. He was peckish.

Mrs Shufflebottom wouldn't make a great meal, Charlie thought. *She's all wrinkly dry skin and brittle bones. But a couple of those children – now they would make a delicious snack. Juicy, tender children. Yum . . .*

His mouth started watering at the thought of chomping into a small –

WHAT AM I DOING?! WHY AM I THINKING ABOUT EATING CHILDREN?!

YES. TASTY, DELICIOUS-SMELLING CHILDREN.

NO! THIS IS TERRIBLE! I CAN'T EAT CHILDREN.

MAYBE DON'T EAT *ALL* THE CHIL-DREN THEN. MAYBE JUST ONE. NOBODY WOULD MISS JUST ONE SMALL CHILD . . .

NO! STOP! I AM A HUMAN, NOT A BEAR! I! AM! HUMAN!

And with that thought Charlie could, thank goodness, at last feel himself start to change back. He bounded over to his house, round the side, into his back garden, and crouched as far away from the kitchen window as he could.

And before he knew it, he was back to Charlie, and any thoughts of eating children had completely disappeared.

Well, *almost* completely.

★★★

Once Charlie had gathered his thoughts and picked up his school bag, he let himself into his house. His mum and dad were both home and deep in conversation. As soon as he heard them, he forgot about being a bear and wanting to eat children, and remembered his anger about the sign outside the house.

He burst into the kitchen. 'What do you call that outside? That for-sale sign?'

'We're just looking into it, Charlie. Exploring options,' his mum said, holding her hands up.

'Yeah, right!' said Charlie.

'It's true. Nothing's decided yet,' his dad continued. 'As I said, we're still hoping it won't come to selling the house, but we have to think about everything.'

'Hmm,' said Charlie, not believing a word they were saying, and he stormed upstairs to his room, slamming the door behind him.

He lay on his bed, worrying. Not just worrying about the house and being poor – no, on top of that he had a new worry.

A very serious worry.

Something different was happening to him when he changed into an animal.

When he was a cat, he'd licked his own bum. And when he was a bear, he'd wanted to *eat* people. He had looked at those children like normal-Charlie would look at a hot dog.

What was happening to him? Was he losing control of himself?

What would happen if he was with his friends and he turned into a lion? Or if he was with his family and turned into a deadly poisonous scorpion? He wasn't safe to be around.

Charlie's thoughts whirled in his head until he heard his dad shouting from downstairs.

'Charlie! SmoothMove! Quick! Come and have a look at this!'

Charlie began trudging downstairs, still angry about the for-sale sign. He met SmoothMove coming out of the sitting room. They shrugged at each other and wandered into the kitchen.

'Come here!' his dad urged. 'I don't believe it!'

His mum and dad were watching the news on the television. Charlie had to stifle a yelp when he saw what was on the screen. Even

SmoothMove was wide-eyed with surprise.

It was shaky mobile-phone footage of a residential street that Charlie knew very well.

And a polar bear.

'That's our road!' his dad exclaimed. 'Can you believe it?'

'Sshh!' his mum said. 'Listen!'

'This shaky but extraordinary mobile-phone footage was taken just a short while ago by a brave, though some might say foolhardy, schoolgirl,' said the news presenter over the footage of Charlie the bear lumbering down the street.

'Quite where the polar bear came from, or – more worryingly – where it has gone, is still a complete mystery. If you do see the creature, do not approach. It could be extremely dangerous, and was said to be looking at a group of terrified schoolchildren as if they were hot dogs. What could have turned into tragedy, though, was averted, as the bear, possibly startled by the childminder Mrs Shufflebottom's brave attempts to frighten the bear and save the children, ran off and attempted to hide behind a tree.'

The footage now showed Charlie trying to hide behind his tree, very clearly visible behind the thin trunk.

'Although judging by this oversized beast's comical attempts to conceal itself,' the news reporter continued, 'it looks like we are dealing here with a bear of *very* little brain.'

Finally the film showed Charlie disappearing round the side of his house into the back garden.

'That's our garden!' shouted his dad. He ran to the patio window and looked out. 'Nothing there now!'

Charlie's mum looked at his dad in disbelief. 'Course it's not still there! Where do you think a great big polar would be hiding? Behind a plant pot?'

Charlie's dad ignored the wisecrack. 'Can you believe it, boys? A polar bear in our back garden!'

'That's quite unbelievable,' said SmoothMove flatly, staring pointedly at Charlie. 'Now *where* could a polar bear have appeared from?'

Charlie shot a warning glance at SmoothMove. Charlie had told his brother about his changing when SmoothMove was in hospital and clearly he hadn't forgotten.[6]

'It's crazy!' said Charlie, trying to sound as disbelieving as he could. 'It must be some kind of trick.'

'And you didn't see anything?' said his mum, looking at them both with an unreadable expression on her face. 'It would have been just about the time you were coming home from school.'

---

[6] Which is totally unsurprising, when you think about it. Finding out that your brother keeps changing into animals isn't the sort of thing you forget in a hurry.

SmoothMove shook his head.

'Nope,' said Charlie. 'Not a thing . . .'

★★★

The next day in school, Charlie didn't have to wait to tell his friends what had happened. The minute he walked into the class they all surrounded him. Well, almost all of them – Wogan was in a corner talking to Daisy again.

'That bear *had* to be you, Charlie!' said Mohsen. 'No question.'

'Good grief, Charlie!' said Flora. 'What happened?'

Charlie explained how seeing the for-sale sign outside his house had made him so stressed that he had changed into a polar bear, although he left out the part about wanting to eat the children. He was too ashamed and worried to share *that*.

'Try not to worry too much about the house,' Flora said, concern in her eyes. 'We'll think of something to help you. OK?'

Charlie gave Flora a small thankful smile. He didn't believe for a second that she'd be able to help, but it was nice to know he had friends who wanted to at least try. The smile disappeared just as soon as it appeared, though.

'Now everybody in the school will know I'm having to move because we're poor,' Charlie said, looking at his feet.

'Charlie, the nice people in school won't care! And the few idiots like Dylan – well, they're idiots so who cares what they think? Forget them.'

'But what if I have to move schools? You'll all forget *me*!'

Flora gasped. 'We will not!'

'No way!' Mohsen blurted, aghast. 'No way would we!'

'Charlie, don't ever think that,' said Flora firmly. 'We are best friends and we would never forget you!'

'I'm sorry, guys,' said Charlie, feeling a little shamefaced. 'I know. It's just sometimes I feel all this bad stuff just happens to me and nobody else. My brother being ill. All the changing. Then this house thing.'

'I know, Charlie. It's rubbish luck. It's totally not fair. But you're the strongest boy I know and I think you're amazing.'

Flora gave Charlie a little hug, and Charlie tried to wipe his eyes without anybody seeing.

A moment later, Wogan wandered over looking a bit pale. 'Hey, what's up, Charlie? See you turned into a polar bear yesterday.'

'That's right. I was just saying –'

'So, that's great but I need a favour,' Wogan interrupted. 'An urgent one.'

'Course,' replied Charlie. 'What is it?'

'I need you to turn into a unicorn.'

'Pardon?'

'I said I need you to turn into a unicorn.'

'You need me to do *what*? *Why*?'

'I need you to turn into a unicorn so I can take a selfie with you. You as a unicorn. It's for a . . . thing. Just something. It's not important why.'

Flora, Mohsen and Charlie all looked at Wogan in various states of disbelief.

'Wogan,' said Charlie slowly, 'I'm not sure unicorns are real. So I really don't think I'll be turning into one. Anyway, why do you need to take a selfie with a unicorn?'

'Gah!' shouted Wogan in frustration. 'So I might have told somebody I could get one.'

'Well, why on earth did you do that?' asked Flora.

'NEVER MIND WHY!' shouted Wogan. 'Stop asking me so many questions!'

He thought for a moment, and then added, 'OK, how about a pony? Can you turn into a pony? A selfie with a pony might do the trick.'

'Look, Wogan,' Charlie said, 'you KNOW it doesn't work like that. I don't get to decide what animals I change into. I don't even get to decide *when* I change into an animal.'

'Maybe you could learn?' suggested Wogan hopefully.

Flora gasped suddenly. 'OH MY GOSH!'

'What?' Charlie said, startled by Flora's sudden outburst.

'Of course!' said Flora. 'Why didn't I think of it before? Wogan, you're a genius!'

Flora reached over, grabbed Wogan and planted a big kiss on his forehead.

'I am?' said Wogan, looking baffled. 'I mean, yes, I am. But why?'

'Because you have just given me an idea!'

'What is it?' Mohsen said, eyes wide. 'Tell us!'

'Not yet,' said Flora. 'It's just an idea. When I've turned it into a plan, I'll tell you.'

'You see,' Wogan said to Mohsen. 'Now *there's* someone who knows the difference between an idea and a plan.'

MWAH!

Mohsen nodded. 'She's a professional.'

'Anyway,' said Wogan, anxiously looking towards Daisy, 'more importantly did anybody see if Daisy noticed Flora kiss me?'

CHAPTER 5

It didn't take long before Flora's idea turned into a plan. She told each of the friends to meet in the playground by the climbing-frame after they had eaten lunch. The four friends wolfed their lunch down as quickly as possible, and rushed outside to the playground.

They stood in a huddle, shivering in the cold. It felt like there was snow on the way. A group of hungry-looking pigeons, pecking at the ground, bobbed nearby. Charlie looked at them suspiciously. Were a couple of them familiar? *No*, Charlie thought. They were just pigeons.[7]

---

[7] In Book 1 there was an incident with some pigeons, and it's highly unsurprising that Charlie was left a little suspicious of them.

'OK,' said Charlie. 'What's the plan?'

'Well,' said Flora, 'it was Wogan who first gave me the idea.'

'So basically I'm the brains here,' said Wogan.

'And it comes from Mohsen's idea as well,' said Flora.

'So basically I am also the brains here,' said Mohsen.

'We are all a part of this plan, guys,' said Flora.

'Apart from Charlie. He's had no ideas,' said Mohsen.

'That's right,' said Wogan. 'Charlie's definitely not the brains here.'

'Guys? Can we listen to what Flora has to say? Please?'

'Thank you, Charlie. So – Mohsen was right. We need to break in to Van der Gruyne Industries and steal back the gold that Dylan's dad stole from Charlie's dad. Then you won't have to sell your home and everything will be back to normal.'

The three boys murmured in agreement.

'The question is *how*? How do four children break in to a high-security office with guard dogs and high walls and guards?'

'And the laser-guided nuclear missiles,' said Wogan.

'No,' said Mohsen. 'We decided the laser-guided nuclear missiles probably didn't exist, remember?'

'We did?' said Wogan. 'Phew! That's awesome news! Strike one to us!' He high-fived Mohsen.

'Anyway . . .' said Flora slowly, 'so how do we break in? It's too difficult for kids. But what happens if we had a special weapon? Maybe a lion that could scare away the dogs? Or a mosquito that could evade security cameras? Or a monkey that could climb over a wall and then open a door? Or a crocodile to bite the security guards?'

'But,' said Wogan, looking a little deflated, 'where are we going to get all those anim— HANG ON A MINUTE! You mean Charlie, don't you?!'

Flora nodded with a sage smile.

'So you think Charlie could change into animals and help the mission?' said Mohsen, his voice laced with excitement.

'*Exactly!*' said Flora.

'OK,' said Charlie.

What Charlie was really thinking but didn't say, was how the thought of changing into an animal filled him with utter dread. What if his new problem got worse and he totally forgot who he was and stayed as an animal forever? He tried to squash the problem away deep down inside himself.

'I don't want to spoil the party here, guys,' Charlie continued, 'but there's a couple of big problems with your plan. Firstly, as we all know, I can't choose which animals I turn into.'

'I realize that,' said Flora. 'We are going to have to improvise.[8] Whatever animal you turn into, we can use its powers. If you're a snake, you can slink through the fence and bite the guards. If you're a worm, you can crawl underground and then right into the building. All animals have their uses.'

'Hmm. OK. But you're forgetting the main problem,' said Charlie.

'Which is?' said Mohsen.

'It's that Charlie can't choose *when* to change,' replied Flora.

---

[8] 'Improvise' means to make things up on the spot, and being able to improvise is a very good thing. So if your teacher asks you why you haven't done your homework, and you can quickly make up a reason, such as 'Aliens broke in to the house and thought my homework was toilet roll and they wiped their massive green alien bum-tentacles on it', then that is improvising. Some might call it 'lying', but that's because they haven't got the imagination to improvise.

'Exactly. I can't just click my fingers and change whenever I want,' said Charlie.

'That,' said Flora, holding a finger up, 'is exactly how Wogan gave me a brainwave.'

Wogan beamed proudly.

'He asked if you could learn how to control when you change,' Flora said, crossing her arms. 'And I think you can. I think we can train you to change when *you* want.'

'Now THAT is a plan,' said Mohsen, wide-eyed with admiration. 'Do that and you really will be a proper superhero.'

'Awesome,' said Wogan, shaking his head in wonderment. 'So, so awesome.'

'And how exactly do you think you're going to train me?' asked Charlie doubtfully.

'I'll show you, but we'll need privacy and quiet. So we all need to arrange a play date at one of our houses on Saturday afternoon. Agreed?'

'Agreed,' said Mohsen immediately.

'Afraid there might be a *teensy* bit of a problem with that actually,' said Wogan. 'There's a My Little Pony movie out this weekend that I thought I'd try to see with Daisy. Apparently Twilight Sparkle pony nearly loses all her powers and –'

'WOGAN!' said Flora.

'Yes?'

'The My Little Pony movie can wait. Charlie needs our help.'

'Gah, OK! I guess it can wait until it comes out on DVD. Then Daisy can come to mine for a play date and we can watch it together. We can get popcorn and marshmallows. Daisy loves marshmallows.'

'Great,' said Flora, looking slightly exasperated. 'Charlie? You up for it?'

Charlie thought for a moment, looking hard at the ground. Saving his family versus the risk of changing into an animal forever? What a decision.

Pigeons circled round them, getting closer. One of them had a foot like a piece of popcorn.

'OK,' he said, swallowing his fear. 'OK. It's worth a go. Let's do it.'

'Yes!' said Mohsen. 'Awesome! So much awesome. There really is no end to the awesomeness in our lives!'

'Excellent,' said Flora. 'Then it's all agreed. We meet on Saturday . . .'

***

It was a long wait for the weekend to arrive. Time seemed to drag endlessly. Charlie thought time had passed slowly when he was forced to watch Mohsen and Wogan play a best-of-seventeen chess match (especially as Mohsen had to teach Wogan how to play as they went along), but the days before the weekend crawled even worse than that. The wait was made all the more miserable because every time Dylan saw Charlie, he had a new cutting comment to throw at him, each one designed to tighten Charlie's stress.

'Anyone bought your house yet, McGuffin?'

Or

'Maybe you could turn into a snail, then you'd never lose your home again.'

Or

'Hey! Charlie! You're . . . you're a great big idiot-head.'[9]

Or

'Hey, Charlie! You're so poor you're going to be homeless! Just in time for Christmas too! Maybe we should get a collection going for you?'

That one hurt. Charlie knew he shouldn't care about being poor, but his ears glowed red with embarrassment – he couldn't help it. It made it worse that Dylan was rich. His house even had a swimming pool. That made it even more unforgivable that Dylan's dad had stolen Charlie's dad's gold – he didn't even need it.

The weekend came eventually, though. They'd arranged the play date for three o'clock at

---

[9] Even Dylan knew this wasn't one of his best.

Charlie's house. By half three, Flora (wearing a hairband with wolf ears) and Mohsen (not wearing a hairband with wolf ears) had arrived, but there was no sign of Wogan (who knows whether he will be wearing a hairband with wolf ears).

Flora jumped up in frustration. 'Argh! Where *is* he? If he's gone to that flipping pony movie with Daisy, I will hang him up by his –'

The doorbell rang just before Flora was able to finish saying exactly what she would hang Wogan up by. A moment later, Wogan walked into the bedroom looking very sorry for himself.

'Sorry I'm late, guys,' said Wogan.

'What's with the gloomy face?' asked Mohsen.

'Ah, don't ask,' said Wogan.

'Oh, what's up? Is it to do with Daisy?' asked Flora, the previous anger on her face replaced with concern.

'No! Seriously. Don't ask,' said Wogan, shaking his head slowly.

'Go on, Woge. You can tell us,' said Charlie. 'What's the problem?'

'OK. Well, I was running late,' said Wogan. 'So I had to rush here. I really needed a poo before I left home but I didn't have time. I was desperate, though, in the car. So on the way we stopped at a restaurant for me to go, but by the time I got to the toilet the poo had gone back up my bum. I tried to poo but I couldn't do it. I missed my poo chance. And I don't know when it will happen again.'

A stunned silence hit the friends.

Mohsen put a reassuring hand on Wogan's shoulder. 'I am so sorry that has happened to

you,' Mohsen said. 'To lose a poo is a terrible thing. We are here for you, my friend.'

Flora and Charlie couldn't put their thoughts into words.

'Thanks, guys. It means a lot to hear that from you,' Wogan said. 'Anyway, how's it all going here? Have I missed anything?'

'No . . .' said Flora. 'You haven't missed anything. Because we've been waiting for you. But you were late.'

'Because of my poo.'

'Because of your poo. Yes. Anyway. Shall we begin?' asked Flora.

'Yes. Please. *Anything* to stop us talking about Wogan's poo,' said Charlie.

'OK, so,' said Flora, 'let's go back to basics. Charlie, what makes you turn into animals?'

'Stress,' said Charlie.

'And what helps you turn back?'

'Deep breathing, relaxing, thinking happy

thoughts, that sort of stuff.'

'OK,' said Flora. 'What happens if you TRY to make yourself stressed by thinking about bad stuff and forgetting all the good stuff?'

'What? Are you mad? That sounds awful,' said Charlie.

'No! It's genius!' said Mohsen. 'I bet if you *made* yourself think bad thoughts, you would definitely change!'

'But I don't want to think bad thoughts! Any bad thoughts I have I like to imagine putting in a little black box and burying them deep, deep down inside myself. And then forgetting about them.'

'Charlie, if you have bad thoughts, you really shouldn't bury them away,' Flora said. 'It's not good for you. Sometimes facing up to bad thoughts is very hard, and you need to be brave. But it's like facing a dragon. If you run away from a dragon and pretend it's gone, it doesn't just disappear – it's still there, burning villages and eating people. But if you face up to it, then you have a fighting chance of beating it. And it's the same with bad thoughts. So hopefully all this will help you face up to your dragon, Charlie.'

'So you're saying that –'

'Guys, really sorry but the poo's back,' said Wogan. 'Don't mean to interrupt but I don't want to miss another –'

Flora glared at Wogan. 'JUST. GO!'

'OK, sorry.' Wogan started tiptoeing out. 'Sorry, sorry, sorry. I'll be as quick –'

'GO!'

Wogan ran out of the room.

Fifteen minutes later, he trotted back in, to a room full of impatient stares.

'Sorry! Took a bit longer than I hoped. Lot of wiping and –'

'JUST SIT!' shouted Flora. 'And *please*. Shush. I mean, honestly!'

Wogan sat
down, giving
everyone a
nervous smile.

'Now. OK.
Hopefully without any
more interruptions, shall
we begin?' asked Flora.
'Are you ready, Charlie?'

Charlie felt sick –
he realized that he was
far from ready.

He was putting his
friends in danger.

Terrible danger.

He'd nearly eaten those children
when he was a polar bear. He couldn't take the
risk.

He couldn't go through with it.

'I'm sorry, guys. I can't do this.'

Mohsen gasped. 'What? Why not?'

'There's something I'm not telling you. And it's putting you in big danger.'

'What danger? What are you talking about?' asked Flora, bewildered.

Charlie swallowed nervously. 'OK, so when I change I . . . I keep forgetting who I am. I'm becoming more and more like the animals I change into. That's why I tried eating a leaf and licked my bum when I was a cat. And –' Charlie hung his head in shame – 'I didn't tell you. But when I was a polar bear I nearly ate some children. They looked delicious.'

The friends sat in silence, taking in this new bombshell.

'So,' said Flora, 'you felt like you were forgetting what it was like to be human?'

'Yes! Exactly! And what happens if I turn into a tiger now and forget who I am and try to eat you?'

'That's a good point,' said Mohsen. 'I don't want to be eaten by a tiger.'

'Or a lion,' said Wogan.

'Or a jaguar,' said Mohsen.

'Or a cheetah,' said Wogan.

'We get the message!' said Flora. 'You don't want to be eaten by –'

'Or a piranha,' said Wogan.

'Don't worry,' said Mohsen, putting a reassuring hand on Wogan's shoulder. 'One piranha flapping on the floor won't be able to eat you, Woge.'

'Phew! Good point. Charlie, you're OK to turn into a piranha.'

'CAN YOU TWO STOP?' shouted Flora.

'They're right, though, Flora,' said Charlie. 'There's too many dangerous animals. It's too risky.'

'Nonsense!' said Flora, smiling at Charlie. 'We just need some protection.'

Flora jumped up and began running around Charlie's room, gathering all sorts of objects and throwing them at Wogan and Mohsen: an American football helmet, a battered old hockey mask, a padded Batman suit, cricket pads, a baseball bat, a catapult and a Nerf gun.

'There,' she said when she'd finished, panting. 'For protection.'

Mohsen turned to Charlie. 'You sure it's necessary?'

'Definitely. Put the stuff on. And if I turn on you, do whatever it takes to stop me and save yourselves.'

A silent, unspoken agreement met Charlie's warning.

After Flora, Mohsen and Wogan had got suited up in protective armour and had their weapons at the ready, Flora continued. 'OK, Charlie, I want you to lie down on the floor. On your back.'

Charlie did as he was told. The three friends sat round him.

'Now, close your eyes.'

Charlie obeyed again.

'Right, now I want you to start thinking about all the bad things you worry about.'

'Really?'

'Yes. Close your eyes again. Think about all your worst fears.'

'Like what?'

'That's not for me to tell you.'

'I'm not sure what to think.'

'What about Flora falling in love with Dyl–'

'It's not for any of us to tell him what to think about, Wogan!' interrupted Flora hotly. 'Only you know what bothers you most, Charlie. But you need to face these thoughts square on. Don't try to control them. See where they take you.'

'OK. I think I've got one.'

Charlie felt for the stress in his belly – there it was, squirming away. Slowly his head filled with thoughts of moving into Aunt Brenda's cat-filled house all the way on the other side of town. He imagined transferring to Huntsman's School for Boys, full of huge trouser-less rugby-playing boys. He imagined being far away from his friends.

Charlie felt electricity start to spark through him.

Another thought jumped out – being caught changing into an animal. Being taken away from his family to be examined by scientists, locked in a hospital, like his brother had been.

Charlie could feel it working. He was changing.

And then his mind twisted towards his new, deepest fear – the fear that he was going to change and forget who he was. Forget that he was Charlie and stay trapped as an animal forever . . .

'Look!' said Mohsen. 'It's starting! He's shrinking!'

The moment Charlie heard the words, though, the change slowed and he started changing back.

'Argh! I nearly had it then! You interrupted me!' said Charlie, infuriated.

'Mohsen!' said Flora.

'Mohsen!' said Wogan, relieved it wasn't him who had got in trouble – he had just been about to shout exactly what Mohsen had done, but Mohsen had beaten him to it.

'Sorry, guys! I was just caught up in the moment,' said Mohsen.

'And you don't have to keep pointing that catapult at me the *whole* time, you know, Wogan,' said Charlie. 'I'm not about to attack you now.'

'It's for protection!' said Wogan, eyes narrowing. 'And anyway, that's exactly what somebody who was about to attack me would say . . .' he continued, stretching the catapult even further back.

'Try to ignore them, Charlie. Let's go for it again,' said Flora.

Charlie lay down and closed his eyes. He tried to summon the dark thoughts again but it was no use.

'I can't do it. It's gone.'

'Just like Wogan's poo,' said Mohsen, nodding wisely.

'Thank you, Mohsen,' said Flora. 'Please, Charlie. Just keep trying.'

'OK . . .'

As Charlie lay there, desperately trying to change, he realized that it wasn't the fact that he had been interrupted that was the problem. It was the fact that Mohsen's familiar voice had reminded Charlie that he was surrounded by friends. Friends that would do anything for him. Even risk being attacked by a tiger. And how could he be stressed when he was with friends like that?

'Guys, I think I need to be alone. I don't think I can get properly stressed with you here.'

'You have to, Charlie,' said Flora gently. 'If we are going to break in to Van der Gruyne Industries, you'll have to do it with us around. Just try again. Think of your dad.'

'And the gold!' said Mohsen.

'OK. I'll try again.'

Once again, Charlie closed his eyes. He breathed deeply. But Charlie had an inkling there was something else holding him back.

'But what about if I forget who I am? For good this time? What about if I don't change back?'

Flora patted Charlie on the arm reassuringly. 'We'll be right here with you. We'll do everything we can to help. Just try to change back as quickly as possible. Then I'm sure you won't have time to forget who you are. OK?'

Charlie took a deep breath. 'OK . . . Here goes nothing.'

CHAPTER 6

Once again, Charlie thought about all his worst fears.

As he breathed out, his friends disappeared from his mind.

He was alone.

His dad's company, McGuffin & Sons,[10] had collapsed . . .

His family had moved to Aunt Brenda's cat-wee-smelling house . . .

He had started at a new school, full of threatening, angry faces . . .

His brother was ill again, stuck on a drip in hospital . . .

[10] Charlie's dad had named his company McGuffin & Sons in the hope that one day his sons would take it over. His hopes of that had faded as both of them switched off as soon as he tried explaining what the company did.

He had changed and became stuck, doomed to stay forever as a tiny, squirming maggot, forgetting that he had ever been a boy called Charlie . . .

Electricity shot through him, from his neurons[11] to his fingertips.

[11] What's a neuron? Well, how am I supposed to know? I think it's a type of smelly Dutch cheese. I'm not sure really. What do you mean I'm the author and I'm supposed to know? FINE – I'll go and look it up. One minute . . .

Right – turns out it's nothing to do with cheese. So apparently neurons are tiny cells in your brain and they make electrical signals that send messages to other cells in your body and tell them what to do. That makes more sense than cheese actually. Neurons are basically the bosses of your body, ordering everybody around. A bit like parents. Or teachers. But if you didn't have any neurons, you'd be about as clever as a piece of wet broccoli.

His body began folding in on itself, like a flower at night.

He was changing and nothing was going to stop it this time.

He was growing smaller, sprouting fur.

Feet turning into paws.

There was a snout. And claws.

He had changed but he had no idea what into.

'FLAMING NORA!' cried Wogan, still aiming the catapult at Charlie.

'HOLY MAJOLY!' exclaimed Flora, staring at him in astonishment.

'I'M GONNA PUKE!' croaked Mohsen.

'Mohsen! Don't be rude!' said Flora.

Yes, thought Charlie. *Don't be so rude!*

'But it was so gross!'

'Yes, it was,' said Flora. 'It was *disgusting* to watch, but it's rude to point it out.'

Guys, thought Charlie. *I can still understand you, you know.*

'I just can't actually believe my eyes,' said Mohsen, who just couldn't actually believe his eyes.

'You've really changed,' Wogan added, almost not believing it had happened right there in front of him. 'I almost can't believe it happened right here in front of me.'

'You did it, Charlie!' said Flora triumphantly. 'Well done!'

She gave Charlie's fur a tentative rub, and then wiped her hand on her dress.

Yes, I know I've changed, thought Charlie, *but can someone* please *tell me what exactly I have changed* into?

'OK, Charlie, it's time to change back before you start forgetting who you are,' said Flora briskly. 'Meanwhile,' she continued, looking at Wogan and Mohsen, 'the important thing is not to startle Charlie *in any way*. You know. In case he . . . erm . . .'

Flora left her sentence hanging, glancing at Charlie with a meaningful look on her face.

No, I don't know! In case I what?! thought Charlie. *What* am *I?*

'Any loud noises or sudden movements might mean he accidentally –'

A sudden knocking sound made everybody jump.

'Everything OK in there?' shouted Charlie's mum through the bedroom door.

'Everything's fine, Mrs McGuffin!' said Flora quickly.

Charlie started panicking and attempted to scurry under the bed but found to his dismay that he couldn't quite fit.

Charlie's mum tried opening the door, but fortunately Flora had had the foresight to jam it, using a Lego model of the *Millennium Falcon* as a doorstop.

'Is this door stuck, kids? Can you let me in?'

Charlie's mum rattled the handle.

Fumbling to put the catapult away, Wogan accidentally let go of the elastic. A small pebble shot from it and hit Charlie squarely on his furry backside.

Charlie yelped in pain and without him even thinking about it, something sprayed *out* of his furry backside. Something that smelled so vile, so nose-bustingly disgusting, that Flora, Mohsen and Wogan immediately started retching.

Charlie finally realized – too late by far – what animal he had changed into. Charlie was a *skunk*.

And he had just blasted his room with maximum-strength skunk spray from his bum.[12]

---

[12] Skunks don't actually spray bad smells out of their bums. They spray out of two little holes either side of their bum called glands. The smell can be so bad it can be detected 3.5 miles away and is strong enough to make fully grown bears run away in terror. What do you mean that's too much information?

'Oh, it's awful,' gagged Wogan. 'I'm going to be sick!'

'No!' said Flora, holding her nose. 'You can't! If you do – oh my goodness it smells SO bad – if you do that, then Charlie's mum will – oh gosh, I think *I'm* going to be sick.'

Mohsen was desperately trying to open the window one-handed, while covering his mouth

and nose tightly with the other. He was looking very pale and trying not to vomit.

Charlie shuffled around, not knowing what to do with himself. Should he hide? Would it be worse for his mum to come in and find Charlie missing or to come in and find him replaced with a skunk?

'What *is* going on in there?' Charlie's mum asked. She tried pushing the door again, but fortunately the *Millennium Falcon* held.

'Nothing, Mrs McGuffin,' said Flora. 'We're just – hurrrgggghhhhhohgod – playing a game.'

'Well, can I just see what you're up to, please?' Charlie's mum pushed the door harder. It cracked open a centimetre.

'No!' shouted Wogan. 'It's a – hurrrghhhogghhhohboy – secret game!'

'Charlie? What's going on in there?'

'Charlie can't talk right now,' shouted Flora. 'He's doing a sponsored si-hurrrrghhhhhhh-lence.'

'A *what*?' shouted Charlie's mum. 'Why are you all making strange noises?'

'A sponsored –' Flora swallowed, concentrating on not heaving – 'silence.'

Holding her nose, she whispered to Charlie urgently, 'Now would be a very good time to change back!'

Charlie closed his little skunk-eyes and desperately tried to slow his breathing and think happy thoughts, but if you have ever desperately tried to calm yourself down, you'll know it's tough. Especially with the sound of your three best friends gagging and heaving, and your mum banging on the door and about to discover you have changed into a skunk.

'Good grief!' shouted Charlie's mum. 'What *is* that smell? Open this door immediately!'

Charlie could see his mum's nose poking round the door. He couldn't help it – he panicked and another blast of foul stench shot out of his bum glands.

Flora looked like she might faint. Wogan for some reason had put Charlie's bin on his head in a vain attempt to protect himself from the smell. By the sounds he was making from inside, it wasn't working.

Mohsen finally managed to push open the

window and mustered the strength to reply. 'Really sorry, Mrs McGuffin, but Wogan just farted.'

Flora, Charlie the skunk and Wogan, still with the bin on, all swung their heads towards Mohsen.

'Farted?' Flora hissed to Mohsen in disbelief.

Mohsen shrugged. 'It was the first – huggghhhhhhh – the first thing that came into my head!'

'Wogan's *farted*?!' said Charlie's mum through the door. 'Good god, the boy needs to see a doctor. It's absolutely terrible!'

'Yeah, sorry, Mrs McGuffin,' said Wogan. 'I had –'

'Take the bin off your head, Wogan!' Flora whispered. 'She won't be able to hear you!'

'Oh yeah,' said Wogan, taking the bin off his head. 'Sorry, Mrs McGuffin – hueggghcccchhhh – I had baked beans for lunch. And beans –

huegggggchhh – for tea last night. Basically I've been eating a load of beans recently. Dad calls me the Human Bum Trumpet.'

'A human bum what?' said Charlie's mum.

'Bum Trumpet.'

'Well, I'm not coming in there with *that* smell, that's for sure. Tea is in twenty minutes. And one thing's for certain: I will *not* be cooking baked beans,' Charlie's mum said. 'And open a window. In fact, open all the windows. It smells like you've got a skunk stashed in there.'

And at the sound of Charlie's mum's feet clomping down the stairs, the four friends let out a collective sigh of relief.

'Now THAT was close,' said Mohsen.

'WAY too close,' agreed Flora.

'Can you pass me the bin again? I'm actually going to puke,' said Wogan. Flora quickly threw the bin at Wogan, who immediately started retching into it.

Wogan's voice echoed from inside the bin. 'Oh boy, the smell isn't getting better!'

'It most certainly isn't,' said Mohsen. 'In fact, I think it might be getting worse. But still – not as bad as one of Wogan's farts.'

Flora started to smile. She looked at Mohsen, who couldn't help but smile back. And then Flora started to giggle. And then Mohsen started to giggle. And then they were both laughing.

The sound of their laughter rushed through Charlie's body, and then he could feel his own laughter bubbling up in reply, and then the laughter started to turn into electricity, fizzing and rippling through his veins. And before Flora and Mohsen's stunned eyes (but not Wogan's, whose head was still in the bin), Charlie changed back from a skunk into Charlie.

He was still laughing until he breathed in the stench he had created.

'Oh my god – huaargh – it's so bad! I couldn't smell it when I was a sku-huuuuuuurrrrgh-nk. Now I know what you were all complaining about. Oh, it's disgusting!'

The other three had run to the open window and were trying to breathe in the crisp, clean air from outside. Charlie got up from the floor and joined them, wiping tears of laughter from his eyes.

Flora clapped him on the back. 'Well, you did it!' she said. 'You changed when YOU decided. I think that officially makes you a superhero.'

'What, Skunkman?' said Wogan. '"Don't make me stinky. You won't like me when I'm stinky"?'

Mohsen laughed. 'With great power comes great stinkability.'

'Yeah, very funny, guys,' said Charlie, grinning.

'Seriously, though. Charlie – this is momentous. But from here on in, the hard work begins.'

'How d'you mean? I've done it, haven't I?

And I didn't forget who I was!'

'You've done it ONCE, Charlie. And that took time for you to get it right. And it took a while for you to change back. You need to practise so you can do it straight away and under pressure. If we're breaking in to Van der Gruyne Industries, we can't be standing around waiting for you to change. And we can't wait around for you to change back from a slug if we're getting chased by ferocious security dogs. So you need to practise, practise, practise. You have to work hard.'

'Totally. Work hard. I'm a hard worker. Everyone knows that.'

'Charlie. What did Mr Wind say in your last school report?'

'I . . . er . . . can't remember.'

'Yes, you can. We all can. Wogan? Mohsen? You both remember?'

Wogan and Mohsen both nodded their heads.

'"Charlie is incredibly lazy and works as little as possible",' said Mohsen.[13]

'OK, OK! I take your point,' said Charlie. 'I'll practise changing every day!'

'Good,' said Flora.

'But what happens if I, you know, start forgetting I'm Charlie again?'

'Did you forget at *any* point while you were a skunk that you were really Charlie?'

'No . . . I guess not,' admitted Charlie.

'Well, there you go then. You've worked out in your brain how to keep hold of the Charlie part of you. You've cracked it.'

'Are you *sure* about that?' asked Wogan. 'Because I –'

---

[13] This is a hundred per cent true comment from this author's school report. Well, look at me now, Miss Twomey! You might have had a good laugh at my expense when you were writing it, but I bet you're not laughing now you're reading this book! Well, actually, I hope you *are* laughing while you're reading this book. YOU KNOW WHAT I MEAN!

'Oh, Wogan,' interrupted Flora sympathetically. 'Of *course* I'm sure.'

But for once, Flora was wrong. Very wrong.

And even more extraordinarily Wogan was right.

CHAPTER 7

'I can't . . .' said Flora, shaking her head.

'I can't . . . actually . . . believe . . .' said Flora, still shaking her head.

'I can't . . . actually . . . believe . . . I was *wrong*,' said Flora. She was never going to stop shaking her head.

'Oh, you get used to it,' said Wogan. 'Believe me. I'm something of an expert.'

It was Monday morning and the friends were sitting in their classroom waiting for Mr Wind to arrive. He was now back from his intensive three-day strategy course with Miss Fyre and was going round the school with a permanent smile plastered on his face.

'But you were *right*, Wogan. I was *wrong* and you were *right*. It's just . . . I don't know what . . .'

'I understand, Flora,' said Wogan, his voice full of tender concern. 'You feel like the world has turned on its head and you don't know what to believe any more?'

'Yes,' said Flora simply, *still* shaking her head.

'I feel the same, Flora,' Wogan said. 'So let's just try to move forward and forget this ever happened. It will probably never, ever happen again.'

Ironically, Wogan was right once more.

'So,' continued Wogan. 'Pull yourself together, Flora. We need you.

Charlie needs you. Look at him.'

They all turned to look at Charlie, who was hanging off the top of the classroom door with one hand while scratching his bum with the other.

'I need you to fix this, Flora,' said Charlie. 'And *then* we need to steal some gold.'

'Steal some *what* did you say?'

Dylan had walked up to them when they weren't looking.

'None of your beeswax, Van der Gruyne,' said Mohsen.

'Yeah, if you think we're gonna tell you about our plan to steal Charlie's dad's gold back from your dad's office, you've got another think coming,' said Wogan firmly.

Charlie, Flora and Mohsen all slowly turned their heads to Wogan, their mouths flapping like goldfish.

'What?' asked Wogan. 'Why are you all looking at me like that?'

'Brilliant.' Dylan rubbed his hands together. 'Thanks for that, Wogan.'

'Thanks for what?' asked Wogan. 'Why is everybody acting so weird?'

'Speaking of weird,' said Dylan. 'What's with him?' He jerked a thumb at Charlie, still hanging off the door.

Good question, Dylan. So what had happened? Why had Flora been so wrong? What had Wogan got right? And why was Charlie hanging off the classroom door scratching his bum?

Well, to find *that* out, we need to do a flashback. Strap yourselves in. Here it comes . . .

We're going back in time . . .

One day . . .

Two days . . .

One hundred and fifty million years . . .

Whoa, that's too far now. We don't want Charlie changing into a diplodocus now, do we?[14]

So, let's go forward in time a bit.

One hundred million years ago . . . Dinosaurs still munching everything . . .

Sixty-six million years ago . . . Still dinosaurs. Jeez, dinosaurs were around for *ages* . . .[15]

---

[14] What do you mean, 'Yes, we do actually. This would be a much better book if it had exciting dinosaur chases and colossal dino-poos'? Look, you don't get to choose what's in the book, OK?

Oh. Apparently, you do. I've just done some research and apparently books with dinosaurs on the cover sell twice as many as books that don't. So – watch out for exciting Dino-Charlie munching action later in this book!

[15] Around sixty-five million years ago there was a giant snake called a Titanoboa. Titanoboas could grow up to 14 metres long, weighed as much as a car and would happily snack on crocodiles. If you're reading this before bedtime, sleep well.

One hundred thousand years ago . . . Finally the dinosaurs have gone but there's cavemen all over the place . . . Can't stop there: Wogan and Mohsen would get hit on the head by big hairy club-wielding Neanderthals . . .

Seven hundred years ago . . . Still too far back: Mohsen and Wogan would probably catch the Black Death . . .

Yesterday . . . That's much better. Hopefully there's nothing around yesterday that would end up with Mohsen and Wogan reaching a sticky end . . .

★★★

Yesterday, Charlie was home and all was reasonably quiet. He had just got out of his seventeenth bath since the skunk incident,[16] and was sitting in the lounge in his dressing-gown. Charlie could

---

[16] The skunk smell had clung to the four friends all weekend. It would be fair to say it had not helped their popularity at school.

hear more barely restrained arguments from the kitchen between his parents about 'company deficit' and 'cash-flow crisis' and other boring stuff that Charlie didn't understand but which still gave him a knot in his stomach.

SmoothMove was on WhatsApp with his new girlfriend. Charlie was considering whether to turn on the PS4 when his parents walked in.

'Guys, can we just have a little word with you?' his mum said.

SmoothMove glanced up from his phone and grunted.

'Well, as you boys know, the house has been up for sale,' his mum continued. Charlie's dad just looked at the floor in silence, an unreadable look on his face. 'And, in fact, we've already had an offer. We've been given some time to think it over, but we need to give the estate agent an answer by the end of next week. So we thought we should let you know.'

'Do you think you're going to accept it?' SmoothMove said.

His dad looked up. 'It's a good offer, son. And we've spoken to Aunt Brenda and she's ready for us.'

And just like that, Charlie felt his world fall apart. It was actually happening. He was leaving his house. Leaving his friends.

SmoothMove grunted again and went back to his phone.

'You OK, Charlie?' his mum asked.

Charlie nodded.

'Sure?' she asked, sitting down next to him and putting an arm round his shoulders.

He nodded again. But he really wasn't. He wanted to shout out 'No! I'm not OK! I'm scared! I don't want Dad's company to go bust and us to be so poor we have to move in with Aunt Brenda! I'm scared my friends will forget me! I'm scared that I'll change to an animal and never change back! And I'm scared SmoothMove will get ill again.'

But telling his parents all that and adding to their stress wasn't going to help matters.

Only one thing was.

He had to get his dad's gold back. And quickly.

And that meant practising changing. Immediately.

Charlie spoke with confidence and positivity that he really wasn't feeling. 'Honestly I'm fine,' he said, trying to disguise a little crack in his voice, and then gave his mum a thin smile. He rushed upstairs and blocked his bedroom door.[17]

He lay down on his floor, toys all cleared away. He propped the big mirror he had borrowed from his parents' room up against the wall – he didn't want to spend any time wondering what animal he had turned into.

It was time to try changing again.

He closed his eyes. He thought of all the stress in his life, which really wasn't difficult. He thought of losing the house, which was fast becoming a reality. He thought of his parents arguing. He thought of rugby in his underpants

---

[17] This was actually the first time Charlie had closed his bedroom door since the skunk incident. Charlie's mum had forced him to keep his windows open all day and night despite the freezing temperatures. She had also made Charlie promise to make sure that Wogan never ate beans before visiting their house ever again.

in the snow. He thought of Mohsen, Flora and Wogan still being best friends with each other but slowly forgetting him . . .

Within a few seconds he could feel the now very familiar static crackle through him.

He started to grow thick fur all over his body. His fingers began to lengthen. He dropped down to all fours and felt his teeth sharpening. Most weirdly of all, he could feel his bum expanding.

As Charlie finished changing, he turned to look at himself in the mirror.

Despite everything he had seen before, what he found there shocked him.

He was a monkey.

But not just any monkey. Oh no.

A monkey with the brightest, biggest and bluest bum he had ever seen.

Ah, thought Charlie. *Not a monkey – I'm a* baboon.[18]

And wow, thought Charlie. *My bottom really is* extraordinary.

Charlie examined his enormous multicoloured behind in the mirror, fascinated, until he finally decided he was actually rather hungry.

A banana, thought Charlie. *That's what I want. A lovely, delicious, yummy banana.*

---

[18] Charlie was close. He wasn't a baboon but a monkey called a mandrill. Baboons and mandrills are totally different animals. The Latin name for a baboon is Giganticus bummus, whereas the Latin name for a mandrill is Spectacula buttox. Mandrills are the world's largest monkey and their bums really are wild and definitely worth a Google.

He began to look around his bedroom, scratching his bum as he did so. *Hmm*, he thought. *No banana. Want banana.*

Charlie realized he needed a poo, and without another thought he squatted down and did one on the floor of his bedroom.

Poo smelly, he thought. *Me no like!*

Charlie jumped off his bed, and scooped it up in his hand. *Me get rid poo. Me throw outside!*

Charlie threw the poo, but it hit the closed window. It slid down the pane slowly.

Charlie watched it, confused, and went up to tap the glass. But he soon lost interest, and began checking himself for fleas instead. He found one and popped it in his mouth. It cracked between his teeth and he swallowed it.

Yummy.

Charlie-Mandrill looked at the top of his wardrobe and decided it looked like a very comfortable place to sit. He jumped on to his bed and swung up to the top of the wardrobe.

Me king of jungle, thought Charlie. *Me swing on vine.*

Charlie jumped off the wardrobe and grabbed the curtain rail, and swung back and forth.

A second later, the curtain rail snapped off the wall, and Charlie crashed to the floor, bringing the curtain and curtain rail down on top of him.

'Charlie!' came a faint call from downstairs. 'Keep that noise down!'

Charlie-Mandrill's ears pricked up as he pulled the curtain off his head.

What that?

'Charlie! Cut that racket out and come downstairs – *Doctor Who*'s on!'

Who Doctor Who? Who calling Charlie?

Charlie . . .

Charlie . . .

He was Charlie.

In a rush it all flooded back to him – who he was, where he was, what he was doing.

It had happened again. He had forgotten everything.

But now he remembered.

'Charlie! It's started! Are you coming?'

It was his mum calling him.

He had to change back fast. He tried to slow his breathing and his thumping heart.

He remembered happy things – laughing with Wogan and Mohsen. Flora. Everything about Flora. Finding out his brother was better again.

He began to change. Relief flooded his body. A moment later, Charlie was Charlie again, a normal boy in a normal bedroom with normal mandrill poo still sliding down his bedroom window.

He had been too close to getting caught – if his mum had decided to come up the stairs instead of shouting . . . Charlie put the thought to the back of his head. He had work to do.

'Down in a minute, Mum! I've just got to do something!' Charlie called.

A minute later, Charlie was ferociously scrubbing clean his window and carpet. He'd worry about what to say about the curtain rail later.

And every so often, without even noticing what he was doing, Charlie would stop to check himself for fleas, disappointed that he couldn't find any. He was still feeling a little peckish.

'Seriously, Charlie,' said Flora. 'Get down from there. Please.'

Charlie glared at Flora, then eventually let go of the classroom-door frame and dropped to the floor.

'Yeah, Charlie,' gloated Dylan. 'Stop *monkeying* around.'

Silence greeted Dylan's joke.

'Yeah . . . and . . .' said Dylan, thinking hard. 'Aaand . . .' said Dylan, still thinking really hard, his face going a little red. 'And it isn't time for acting like a monkey because it's not half past ape.'

An even denser silence greeted Dylan's second joke.

'Half past *ape* . . . It sounds like half past *eight*,' explained Dylan.

'We get it, Dylan,' said Flora flatly.

'Are you OK, Dylan?' said Mohsen.

'Yes! I'm fine! It's him who's not fine!' Dylan pointed at Charlie. 'He's clearly still a bit monkey, isn't he?'

Once again, the friends were silent. They knew Dylan was right.

'So you'd better sort *that* little problem out before you try breaking in to the international headquarters of Van der Gruyne Industries! Oh, and guys,' Dylan continued, 'I'll be telling my dad to lay on extra security. And I'll be watching you.'

And with that Dylan made a rude face and waltzed off.[19]

Wogan thumped his palm in frustration. 'I don't believe it! How on earth does Dylan know all about us breaking in to –' He paused, as a cloud of confusion lifted from his eyes. 'Ah. Yes. I see. *Now* I know why you were all looking at me weirdly before. Sorry about that, guys.'

---

[19] Dylan didn't literally waltz off. Dylan is weird, but he's not that weird. He just walked away.

'It doesn't matter,' said Charlie. 'We can't go through with the plan anyway.'

'What? Why?' cried Mohsen.

'Because I'm never making myself change again. You don't know what it was like. For a minute I *totally* forgot myself. I forgot who I was. Where I was. I forgot my mum and my dad and my brother. Everything. I even forgot about you guys.' Charlie looked glumly at his friends. 'The only thing I could think about was trying to find a banana.'

'Flora,' said Mohsen. 'This is the bit where you say something clever to make everything better.'

'That's the problem, though,' said Flora. 'I haven't got anything. I don't know what to say.'

A grim cloud hung over the friends for about 3.1415926 seconds before Flora piped up.

'Oh, actually . . . Hang on a minute. Charlie – tell me *exactly* what happened before you started remembering who you were?'

'I'm not sure really. All I know is that one minute I was a monkey – or a baboon to be precise[20] – pooing on the floor when I heard –'

'You were whatting, did you say?' said Wogan.

'I was pooing on the floor when –'

'It's been a bad time for you recently,' said Mohsen, full of concern. 'First with the whole licking-your-own-bum thing, and now the pooing on your bedroom floor.'

'Thanks for pointing that out, Mohsen. ANYWAY. The point is I was a *baboon*![21] Baboons don't care where they poo. I wasn't even slightly Charlie any more. And the next thing I remember was my mum was calling me from downstairs about *Doctor Who*.'

'Hmm,' said Flora.

'Look!' said Wogan, wide-eyed and pointing at Flora. 'She's hmming!'

---

[20] Not a baboon. A mandrill. I refuse to correct this again.

[21] Unbelievable. I give up.

'Oh!' exclaimed Mohsen. 'That's always an excellent sign.'

'Exactly!' said Wogan. 'She's on to something. I can feel it.'

'Well, yes, anyway,' said Flora. 'I think –'

'Here it comes!' said Wogan.

'I was about to say,' said Flora. 'I think that –'

'This is very exciting!' squealed Mohsen. 'What's she going to say?'

'STOP! INTERRUPTING! ME! I will – I will – WELL YOU DO NOT WANT TO FIND

OUT WHAT I WILL DO!' Flora shouted, red
in the face. 'DO YOU UNDERSTAND?'

Mohsen and Wogan immediately began
nodding their heads as vigorously as they could,
edging backwards nervously as they did so.

'That's better,' said Flora. 'What I was about
to say was that I think Charlie's mum was the
key. When Charlie was by himself, he started
forgetting who he was. But when his mum
called, her voice reminded him that she was
there. And so she reminded Charlie of who he
was. Who loves him and who he loves. It was

SORREE...

Whoa

when you changed into a skunk, u didn't forget who you were because you were with your friends. And because friends are part of who we are.'

'So, how does that help us?' Charlie asked.

'Charlie!' said Mohsen. 'Don't interrupt her! Please!'

'You forgot who you were, Charlie, because you *felt* you were by yourself. You need to learn to be strong in yourself, no matter if you're completely alone. And until then, we're here for you. You are not to change unless one of us is with you. I think you're safe to change then. So as long as we stick together at the break-in I reckon you'll be OK.'

'You see!' said Mohsen. 'Every time she pulls it out the bag. But hang on . . . What about Dylan? He knows what we're planning now, thanks to bladdermouth over there.'

'I think you mean bla*bb*ermouth, Mohsen. Anyway, well, we'll just have to deal with Dylan if necessary,' replied Flora solemnly.

'OK. So . . . are we back on for the breaking in and the stealing the gold and the saving of the McGuffin house just in time for Christmas?' Wogan asked, looking pointedly at Charlie.

Charlie looked out of the window, his brow furrowed in concentration. The friends hardly dared breathe waiting for his answer.

'OK,' Charlie finally said. 'We're back on.'

'Yes!'

'Awesome!'

'Well done, Charlie,' said Flora, smiling. 'You're the best!'

'OK, then,' said Charlie quickly, trying to hide a blush. 'What's the plan?'

'Right,' said Flora. 'Here it is. We meet first thing Saturday morning –'

'Whoa, whoa, whoa,' said Wogan, holding his hand up. 'Hold on there. I can't do Saturday morning. I've got the Mermaid Club Christmas party.'

'Mermaid Club?' asked Flora flatly.

'Mermaid Club?' asked Charlie even more flatly.

'A club . . . for mermaids?' asked Mohsen. 'But . . . you're not a mermaid.'

'It's not a club *for* mermaids. It's for people who *like* mermaids,' said Wogan.

'Since when do *you* like mermaids?' asked Mohsen.

'Oh, since ages ago,' replied Wogan. 'What's *not* to like? You know, I like their . . . their . . . slipperiness. And stuff.'

'Slipperiness?' replied Mohsen.

'Mmm-hmm,' said Wogan uncertainly.

'And would a certain Daisy be attending this Mermaid Club?'

'Perhaps. But I really don't see what that has –'

'And are there actually any other members of the Mermaid Club apart from you and Daisy?' continued Mohsen.

'I am uncertain of the membership take-up as yet.'

'Yes, well, anyway,' said Flora, ignoring him. 'Saturday afternoon? Can you do that?'

Wogan nodded his head.

'It's not going to affect your love life?' asked Flora.

Wogan shook his head.

'OK, then. That's settled. So, here's the plan. Get dressed in completely dark clothes, and then we meet on Saturday afternoon at two o'clock . . .'

CHAPTER 8

It was Saturday afternoon, at ten past two. Mohsen, Flora and Charlie were waiting round the corner from Van der Gruyne Industries, all with small rucksacks on their backs. Flora had instructed them to each bring a bag with sensible emergency supplies. Flora's bag contained a bottle of water, a torch, a compass, four apples and a whistle. Charlie's had a four-pack of Mars bars and a small collection of pebbles that he'd forgotten to take out. All Mohsen had in his bag was a half-empty sandwich box that he'd been munching through on the way.

They were alternately looking at their watches and down the street. A few mangy-looking pigeons were pecking around them, hunting for crumbs.

The wait for Saturday had seemed interminable for the friends. The closer they got to the day, the more nervous they had become. And now the moment had arrived and their nerves were jangling.

'I will absolutely LOSE my rag COMPLETELY if Wogan doesn't turn up VERY QUICKLY!' Flora seethed.

A moment or two later, Wogan tore round the corner, pedalling furiously on his bike.

'Sorry I'm late, guys,' he puffed. 'I . . . erm . . . forgot I had to . . . erm . . . help my mum with the gardening. So I came straight from doing that.'

Flora eyed Wogan beadily. 'You're not late because you've been with Daisy all day then?'

'No! No way!' Wogan replied, looking indignant at the very suggestion. 'I told you! I've been gardening.'

'Wogan. Tell me. What's that you're wearing on your head?'

Wogan looked blank for a moment, then his hand shot to his head. On his head was a headband, and sticking out of the headband was a huge sparkly silver unicorn horn.

'Ah,' said Wogan. 'Yes. I see.'

'Do you often do gardening dressed as a unicorn?' Flora asked.

'I . . . Yes. I do.'

'And remind me again. Does Daisy like unicorns?'

'Yes,' replied Wogan in a tiny voice just above a whisper.

'Hmm,' hmmed Flora.

'Did you hear that?' said Mohsen, nudging Charlie. 'That's a totally new type of hmm.

It sounded to me like a furious hmm.'

'Not now, Mohsen,' said Wogan, anxiously looking at Flora.

'And tell me,' continued Flora, 'does a sparkly unicorn horn count as dressing in dark clothes?'

'I guess not . . . Should I take it off then?'

'Yes! You should! We are *trying* to be inconspicuous!'

'Oh, Wogan,' said Mohsen, shaking his head sadly. 'This Daisy is really turning your head. You need to keep your eye on the game.'

But Wogan, with a determined look on his face, folded his arms and kept the unicorn horn on his head.

'It is! Has anybody got any water? I'm pretty thirsty after that bike ride.'

Flora handed him her bottle of emergency water. Wogan drained the bottle completely in three gulps and gasped with satisfaction.

'Well, anyway,' said Charlie, as the four

friends began slowly walking towards the side entrance of Van der Gruyne Industries, 'at least he's here now. So, what's the plan, then?'

They all turned to Flora.

'Why are you all looking at me? I've told you my plan. We come here, Charlie turns into an animal, helps us to break in, we steal back the gold, then leave.'

'You . . . er . . . haven't got any more detail than that?' Charlie asked cautiously. 'It's totally fine if you don't!' he added quickly, catching Flora's steely gaze.

'No,' Flora said, 'I don't.'

'You haven't planned beyond this moment?' asked Mohsen.

'Nope,' said Flora.

'So you have no idea what's going to happen and you are hoping it will just come to you as we go along?'

'That's right.'

'You don't think it's quite stressful getting to this point and having no idea what you're going to do next?'

'No!' replied Flora. 'It's actually quite liberating.'

'Well, I hope it all works out in the end,' said Mohsen uncertainly.

'Yes,' agreed Flora. 'So do I.'

'OK,' said Charlie. 'Well, let's look what we have in front of us, and then we can hopefully work out what on earth we are going to do.'

What was in front of them was the towering bulk of Van der Gruyne Industries, a vast grey faceless building with a thousand blank windows staring out. Behind it, ink-black licks of clouds scudded across a darkening steely sky. There was a huge metal fence – so tall that if Wogan stood on Mohsen's shoulders, he would just about be able to reach the top. No good for

climbing over, though, as it was topped with extra-sharp barbed wire. As it was a Saturday, the office was shut, but security guards were patrolling the grounds. Two of them had dogs. Huge German shepherds. Dylan had been true to his word – there did appear to be more guards on duty.

'Well,' said Mohsen after their brief examination of the building, 'after close consideration, it looks like we're stuffed. No way are we getting in there. And even if we somehow did, there's no way of getting out. In short, I vote we call it a day and go home.'

'Mohsen!' shouted Wogan. 'Don't be such a negative nelly!'

Mohsen bristled. 'Do NOT call me a negative nelly!'

'Well, you are!'

'I'm just being practical. And, guys, what we're about to do – it's stealing. It's against the law. We could set a bad example to other children.'

'Look,' said Wogan. 'Think of Robin Hood. When he was stealing from the prince of Nottingham –'

'Sheriff,' corrected Flora.

'Yes, when Robin Hood was stealing from

the prince of Sheriff, he didn't care about setting a bad example to children! He just stole from the rich and gave to the poor. AND he did it wearing tights.'

Flora nodded in agreement. 'Exactly, Wogan. I couldn't have put it better myself. What we are doing is morally correct.[22] Dylan's dad stole the gold off Charlie's dad. It belongs to Charlie's family. We are just getting back what is rightfully theirs.'

'OK,' replied Mohsen in a small voice. 'I don't have to wear tights, do I?'

Wogan put an arm round Mohsen's shoulder. 'No, my friend. You don't. And it's OK to be scared, you know. I'm scared too.'

---

[22] What does 'morally correct' mean? It basically means 'the right thing'. Simple, yes? Well, sometimes doing the right thing isn't so simple. Lying is 'morally wrong' – you are told that from an early age. But what if a friend drew a picture and asked you what you thought of it? It may be a terrible picture, but surely it's better to lie and say it's a wonderful picture? Obviously it is. Just like if you think this book is the worst book you have ever read, it is ALWAYS better to lie and tell everybody you think it is actually the GREATEST book you have ever read and you should also give it the best reviews online because that is the MORALLY CORRECT thing to do. Is that clear? Good.

'So am I,' said Charlie.

'So, we're ALL scared then?' said Mohsen hopefully.

They all turned to Flora.

'Oh. Erm, yes. Absolutely. Scared. Definitely.'[23]

'Hmm,' said Mohsen suspiciously.

'Oh! You hmmed!' said Wogan.

Mohsen beamed proudly. 'So I did!'

'OK, Charlie,' said Flora. 'This is it.'

Flora held one hand flat out, palm up. One by one, they all high-fived her. A nervous tension shivered through them as they looked into each other's eyes.

'It's time,' she continued. 'Charlie, we need you to change into something useful now. Maybe something scary, like a lion. You could jump over the gate and scare all the guards and dogs away. Maybe try to think fierce when you

---

[23] Here's an example of 'morally correct' lying. Of COURSE Flora isn't actually scared – she is lying to make Mohsen feel better.

change? You never know – it might work . . .'

Charlie gulped. 'OK, here goes nothing!'

Charlie closed his eyes and opened his mind. Opened it to all his fears and stresses and worries. In flooded images of moving house . . . the sound of Aunt Brenda's wooden leg rapping on the floorboards . . . the feeling of being alone, without friends . . . memories of a hospital ward with his brother attached to a drip – everything in his life that could go wrong.

It didn't take long for the change to start. As the electricity shot through every nerve of his body, in his mind Charlie pictured lions and tigers and panthers.

He could feel himself changing.

Shrinking.

Shrinking?

Well, that's *not a good sign* . . .

He felt his body being squeezed and crushed. He could feel wings growing, a beak forming, feathers sprouting.

He could feel his feet turning into small clumpy claws.

OK, thought Charlie, *I* really *don't think I'm a lion.*

'Oh, for goodness' sake, Charlie!' shouted Wogan. 'You're a *pigeon*!'

A pigeon! thought Charlie. *Not again* . . .

Mohsen groaned. 'What use is a ratty old pigeon? Change back, Charlie!'

Excuse me! thought Charlie. *How dare you call me ratty* —

''Allo!'

The unexpected voice from behind Charlie startled him.

It was a voice he knew. A French accent he'd heard before.

And it was the very last voice on earth he wanted to hear right now.

'*Sacré bleu*, my pretty little princess! You 'ave finally returned to me!'

Charlie swung round. There, bobbing in front of him, was a pigeon that he recognized very well.

'It is I, Jean-Claude, and –'

'I know who you are,' replied Charlie. 'And can I just say, I am *not* a princess!'

'Prince, princess, who cares with a love like ours? We are modern pigeons. We shall fly off as one. I, Jean-Claude the pigeon, and you, Farley McStuffin!'

'My name's not Farley McStuffin! It's Charlie McGuffin.'

'Zat is what I said! I, Jean-Claude the pigeon, and you, Gnarly EggMuffin!'

'I give up.'

Wogan was staring at the chattering pigeons with growing disbelief.

'Hang on, is Charlie talking to that pigeon? Charlie!' Wogan began to speak very loudly and very slowly. 'Charlie. Are. You. Talking. To. That. Pigeon?'

Jean-Claude sidled up uncomfortably close to Charlie.

''Ow long I have been waiting for you,' he

cooed, 'knowing our star-crossed paths were destined once again to – Ah! What is this? I spy with my *petit* eye some delicious-looking crumbs of pizza crust! I must depart! I bid you adieu, my gorgeous little cauliflower!'

And with that Jean-Claude flapped off a metre or so and began pecking at the ground. Charlie was just gathering his thoughts when Jean-Claude flapped right back next to him.

'Alas! A false alarm,' Jean-Claude cooed. 'It was not pizza crust. It was little stones. Some tiny pebbles, perhaps. The pebbles were . . . not so delicious. No matter. We have not a moment to lose! Let us fly aw–'

A sudden flap of wings announced the arrival of another pigeon.

'*Zut alors!* Can it be true? It is true! You are back! It is I, Antoine the pigeon! Did I 'ear someone mention ze crust of pizza? I do not even like ze crust of pizza, and yet I find it . . .

 irresistible. Like you, Snarly McFluffin.'

'MY NAME IS CHARLIE MCMUFFIN – I MEAN MCGUFFIN!' cooed Charlie as loudly as he could.

'He's definitely talking to them,' said Wogan. 'What's he saying?'

'I'm not sure. I don't speak pigeon,' said Mohsen.

Wogan thumped his palm in frustration. 'Gah! Neither do I!'

Charlie was also becoming increasingly frustrated. He had to change back to Charlie and try to change into a more useful animal, but with the wittering pigeons around him there was no way he could relax enough.

And then an idea struck Charlie like a bolt of very clever lightning.

'Jean-Claude, Antoine? You know how you

are my favourite pigeons in the whole world?'

Jean-Claude bobbed his head, as if giving a little bow. '*Mais oui!* But of course! This is music to my tiny ears.'

'*Mais non!*' cooed Antoine. 'That is not music to *my* tiny ears! You can only have one most special pigeon. You must choose, Harley Bumchuffin –'

'Charlie McGuffin.'

'Yes, that is what I said. You must decide between I, Antoine, the most handsome pigeon in this general area, and Jean-Claude, who is nothing but a pebble-pecking – Oh! A moment! Is this a delicious morsel I spy on the ground? Could it be . . .? Yes! I think it is some tasty seed or perhaps corn of ze pop!'

Antoine pecked something off the ground and chewed it. Jean-Claude flapped over and started pecking at the ground next to Antoine and also began chewing.

'Ah! *Non*. It is not corn of ze pop,' Antoine cooed, spitting out what he had been chewing. 'It was a little piece of dog poo. An easy mistake to make.'

Jean-Claude spat out what he had in his beak, and looked at Antoine with what Charlie could only describe as a pigeon-glare.

'Foolish pigeon!' Jean-Claude cooed angrily. 'This is why you are not to be trusted with the crumbs in this general area. I am the emperor of crumbs and –'

Charlie flapped his wings in exasperation. 'Guys! Guys. Please. Let's focus, OK? You want to make me happy, right?'

Both pigeons bobbed their heads, nodding in agreement.

'*Oui!*'

'*Bien sûr!*'

'Right. Then here's how you can help . . .'

Meanwhile, Flora, Mohsen and Wogan were wondering what on earth was going on.

'Why isn't Charlie changing back?' asked Mohsen.

'I'm not sure, but he certainly seems to be chatting to those other pigeons an awful lot,' replied Flora.

'You don't think he's forgotten who he is, do you?' asked Wogan.

'I'm sure he hasn't,' said Flora. She didn't sound very sure.

'Well, do you think we should remind him?' asked Wogan. 'CHARLIE! YOU ARE NOT A PIGEON! DON'T FORGET YOU –'

Before Wogan could finish his sentence, with a great flap of wings Charlie, Jean-Claude and Antoine took off.

Antoine flew away from the building and out of sight, but Jean-Claude and Charlie soared straight over the heads of Flora, Wogan and Mohsen, who were watching them open-mouthed. They flew over the fence of Van der Gruyne Industries and, like plump grey arrows, went straight for the security guards.

The guards didn't know what hit them.

They had been told by Mr Van Der Gruyne to keep an eye out for a group of children trying to sneak in. What they *hadn't* been told to keep an eye out for was a pair of angry-looking pigeons. So, instead of checking the sky for airborne menaces, they were eating egg sandwiches, texting their boyfriends and girlfriends, picking their noses – anything but looking out for vicious feathery beasts.

Charlie and Jean-Claude dive-bombed the guards, pulling off their hats and pecking at their ears and noses. They grabbed their hair with their claws, pulling and tugging at it. The guards started running in circles, shouting and screaming and waving their arms. A couple of them were even crawling on the ground as they tried to escape.

The dogs were barking excitedly at the pigeons, trying to jump up and catch them in their snapping jaws, but Charlie and Jean-Claude were too agile, swooping out of the way at the last second, which was driving the dogs into an even greater frenzy.

Once the guards and dogs were all in complete chaos, Charlie and Jean-Claude climbed higher, circling above their heads. Then Charlie gave a signal – a single loud coo – and both pigeons released enormous sloppy pigeon poos all over the security guards.

The guards were now running in frantic terrified circles, half of them with poo dripping down their heads, faces and shoulders.

'Success! We have ze cowards on the run!' cried Jean-Claude. 'Ah, ze sweet taste of victory – Oh! What is this? A dropped egg sandwich! I believe it must be sandwich-pecking time!'

Jean-Claude flew down and began a tug of war with the guard's half-eaten sandwich. Charlie landed next to him as the guards, given a brief respite, began to recover themselves, wiping themselves down and picking up their hats.

'Jean-Claude!' cooed Charlie urgently. 'We need to keep attacking the guards, or . . . or . . .'

And suddenly Charlie found that he couldn't quite remember exactly why it was so important to attack the guards.

Ah, well, he thought. *Can't have been that important. Not when there are so many delicious crumbs in the general area.*

And Charlie started pecking at the sandwich crumbs. *Delicious.*

The guards saw that the pigeons, who a moment ago had been attacking them, were now happily snacking on their sandwich remains. With murderous looks on their faces, and with the guard dogs snapping and baying and pulling on their leashes, they approached the pigeons menacingly, clearly intent on revenge.

Flora, who was watching keenly, saw the danger before anybody else.

'Charlie! Wake up! You are not a pigeon! Forget the crumbs!'

The security guards were nearly upon the pigeons. They were fiddling with their dogs' collars, about to release them.

'Oh, Charlie!' Flora cried at the top of her voice. 'Watch out! The guards are coming! Please, Charlie! You're a HUMAN!'

''Ere,' said one of the guards to another. 'Did that kid just call one of these pigeons "Charlie"?'

Charlie heard the voice and cocked his head.

That voice . . . it was Flora! And, in a sudden rush, the sound kick-started Charlie's memory.

The guards released the dogs, and they came hurtling forward, jaws snapping and drooling. Charlie flapped away just in time, the clamping teeth brushing the edge of his tail feathers.

Once they realized Charlie had escaped, the dogs turned sharply and bolted towards Jean-Claude.

'Jean-Claude! Move! Quickly!' Charlie cooed in desperation.

Jean-Claude looked up from the egg sandwich to see the two German shepherds closing in on him.

'Ooh la la!' He flapped into the air at the last second, leaving the dogs snapping at the air below them.

'Alas, I must leave this beautiful sandwich!' Jean-Claude cooed.

The dogs barked and jumped below them,

saliva drooling from their gnashing mouths.

'I fear these dogs are too fierce for us, my *petit* pretty pigeon! And I am without any more poo to drop on the guards! We must beat a hasty retreat!'

With a heavy heart Charlie realized Jean-Claude was right. His plan had failed almost before it had begun.

But then a sudden coo from Jean-Claude changed everything.

'Reinforcements! Look! Behind you!'

Charlie circled round and almost couldn't believe his beady pigeon eyes. A flock of pigeons, dozens and dozens of them, were arrowing towards Charlie and Jean-Claude.

And at the front of the grey cloud was Antoine!

'I bring some 'elp, Barley Yakpuffin!' Antoine cooed. 'Zey come to 'elp me win your heart!'

Jean-Claude, Antoine and the huge flock of pigeons, as if with one mind, soared high into the air and then dropped all at the same instant, dive-bombing the guards, pecking and clawing at their faces. To the faint sounds of cheering from his friends Charlie flew at the guards and joined in.

Antoine cooed once more, and the great flock of pigeons soared into the air, circled, and then again, at exactly the same moment, poo-bombed the guards.

The guards did not know what hit them.

A sea of pigeon poo dropped on to their heads, drenching them, soaking their hair, dripping down their faces and into their eyes and mouths. And that was enough for the guards.

Closely followed by the wildly barking dogs, they started running for cover, but the pigeons wouldn't let them. A whirlwind of biting and scratching and flapping birds pecked and harried and herded the guards – like terrified poo-covered sheep – out of the gate and down the road.

Flora, Wogan and Mohsen whooped as they watched the security guards run off into the distance, desperately trying to escape the assault from the pigeon air force. The sounds of barking echoed in the distance long after the guards had disappeared from sight, leaving the gate wide open and undefended.

A moment later, a single pigeon

flapped back and joined the friends, and, a few seconds after that, Charlie had changed from Charlie the pigeon back to Charlie the boy.

'Now THAT was awesome!' said Mohsen.

'It truly was,' said Flora. 'But we have to keep moving. Let's get inside the building while we can.'

CHAPTER 9

Charlie, Mohsen, Wogan and Flora shot through the open gate and towards the Van der Gruyne Industries building.

'Which way?' shouted Charlie, relieved to be human again, the lingering taste of egg sandwich in his mouth a reminder of how close he had come to getting stuck as a pigeon forever.

Wogan pointed. 'That's the front door, but it's probably locked. If we go round the back, though, there's an entrance into the basement that we might be able to sneak in through.'

His three friends turned to look at Wogan.

'And how on earth do you know that?' asked Flora, eyes narrowed with suspicion.

'Because I came here a couple of years ago on a school trip,' said Wogan matter-of-factly.

'You've been here on a school trip?' said Flora, staring at Wogan. 'And you didn't think of mentioning that before now?'

'I didn't think it was important,' protested Wogan.

'*You didn't think it was important?!* Sometimes I – Never mind. Let's go!'

They skirted round the building until they found some stairs, which led down to a door.

'You don't think the door will be alarmed, do you?' asked Mohsen nervously.

'Definitely not,' replied Wogan, pushing it open.

An ear-splitting alarm shrieked through the whole building.

Wogan shrugged. 'It was a guess, OK?' he

yelled above the noise. 'Not the best guess, I admit.'

'Charlie? Can you do something?' shouted Mohsen, hands over his ears.

'What do you mean, can I do something?' bellowed Charlie.

'What?' replied Mohsen.

'TAKE. YOUR. HANDS. OFF. YOUR. EARS.'

'WHAT?'

'I said,' replied Charlie, pulling Mohsen's hands away from his ears, '"What do you mean, can I do something?"'

'You know, change into an animal and stop the alarm?'

'What sort of animal?' asked Charlie incredulously. 'An alarm-fixing zebra?'

'OK, fair point, I guess not.'

And then, just as suddenly as the alarm had started ringing, it stopped.

'Wow, that is SUCH a relief,' said Wogan.

'Isn't it? I thought my head was going to explode,' said Charlie, grinning.

'What?' said Wogan.

'You can take your fingers out of your ears now, Wogan.'

'But why would the alarm just switch off like that?' asked Flora.

'No idea!' said Charlie. 'Maybe it ran out of batteries.'

'Maybe . . .' Flora didn't sound particularly convinced.

'Where *are* we?'

The four looked around. They were in a dark low-ceilinged basement. Huge banks of computers snaked round the room, all glowing and humming. Some tinsel hung limply on the walls.

'Oh!' said Wogan. 'I remember this room. These are the servers for Van der Gruyne Industries – the computers that store all the important information for the company.'

'OK, then we know where we are, but where do we go?' Flora said.

'I don't know. Wherever they keep their safe, I suppose,' Charlie replied.

'Their safe?' asked Mohsen.

'Well, where else do you think they'd keep the gold?'

'I guess,' Mohsen agreed. 'And how on earth are we going to break in to a safe if we do find it?'

'Charlie's just going to have to use animal strength to bust it open,' Flora replied. 'And my theory is they'd keep a safe in Dylan's dad's office.'

'You're probably right,' agreed Charlie. 'But where is *that*? Wogan – don't suppose you know, do you?'

'No. Sorry,' said Wogan.

'Then we'll just have to search the building,' said Flora.

Mohsen gasped. 'The whole building?' he said. 'That'll take forever! This place is huge!'

'Well, we don't have a choice, do we?' snapped Charlie. 'So let's just get going.'

'Or we could look at the map,' suggested Wogan.

Once more, the others turned to Wogan in unison.

'What map?' asked Flora, eyes narrowed again.

'I forgot to say I googled Van der Gruyne Industries yesterday and found a floor plan on the council website, so I printed it out.'

His three friends stared at Wogan in wide-eyed silence.

'What?' said Wogan. 'Why are you all staring at me like that?'

'Un-be-liev-able,' said Flora. 'Is there anything else you'd like to tell us that you might have forgotten?' she asked.

'How am I supposed to tell you if I've forgotten?'

Even Flora couldn't argue with that logic.

'Well, if anything else important pops into your head –'

'Actually, there is one other thing,' said Wogan.

'What?' asked Charlie.

'I need a wee.'

Flora put her hands on her hips. 'Really? Now?'

Wogan nodded.

'Can't you wait?' asked Charlie. 'It's just things are a little urgent right now. What with us being in the middle of a robbery.'

'I guess . . .' said Wogan, sounding very unsure.

'OK, great then,' said Charlie. 'Now, get your map out. Which way?'

Wogan examined the map, and pointed to the door they had just come through. 'That way!'

'What?' said Mohsen. 'Back outside? You sure?'

Wogan looked at the map again. 'Sorry!' he said, turning the map the right way up. He pointed to a different doorway, which seemed to lead into a long corridor. 'The president's office is on the top floor. The lift is this way.'

They ran down the corridor, and then down another, while Wogan looked at his map and called out instructions.

Finally they turned a corner and arrived at a lift. Mohsen pressed the button. All four nervously looked up and down the corridor, praying that no security guards would appear. After what seemed like an age, the lift pinged, the doors opened and they piled in. Mohsen hit the button for the top floor. The doors slid closed, and the lift started rising.

'This is all a bit too easy for my liking,' Flora thought to herself aloud, which is basically the same as speaking.

'Don't worry!' said Mohsen. 'There's no need to –'

And then the lift suddenly stopped.

Between floors.

The four friends looked at one another, panic etched on each face.

Mohsen hit the button repeatedly.

Nothing.

The lift was completely stuck.

'What do we do?' asked Charlie.

He was met with three blank faces and shrugs.

Mohsen gulped. 'We're trapped.'

'Guys,' said Wogan, 'I don't want to make a bad situation worse, but I REALLY need the toilet.'

Flora stamped her foot. 'WOGAN! Now is NOT the time. We need to focus. How are we going to get out?'

Mohsen tried banging the buttons again, but that didn't do anything.

'Could we reach the emergency hatch?' Mohsen said, pointing to a panel above their heads.

'And then what?' asked Charlie.

'We could all climb out?'

'And then?'

'We could . . . climb the inside of the lift shaft to the next floor?'

'And then?'

'Prise the doors apart?'

'Mohsen,' said Flora firmly.

'Yes?'

'We are nine years old. We aren't going to climb up any lift shafts. Wogan can't even climb the rope at school.'

'That's true actually,' said Wogan, nodding. 'I just sort of get stuck and dangle at the bottom. But seriously, we need to focus on the main problem here – I'm going to wee myself. It's actually going to happen in about thirty seconds.'

'You can't wee on the floor when we are all stuck in here,' said Flora. 'You've GOT to hold on!'

'Twenty-five seconds,' said Wogan, crossing his legs.

'Oh, for goodness' sake!'

'Quick – does anybody have a flask or a bottle he could wee in?' asked Charlie.

'I've got my sandwich box,' suggested Mohsen, with some reluctance. 'But –'

'Fifteen seconds,' said Wogan, slightly bending over, his voice strained.

'QUICK!' shouted Charlie. 'Get it out!'

Mohsen tore open his bag and pulled out his sandwich box . . .

'Ten seconds.'

. . . threw out the remaining sandwiches . . .

'Five seconds.'

. . . and flung the box at Wogan.

'There!'

Quick as a flash, Wogan dropped Mohsen's sandwich box on the floor in the corner, pulled his pants down, and just at the very last second before disaster struck, started doing a wee in it.

Flora, Charlie and Mohsen stared the other way, trying to ignore the wee, which was both ridiculously loud and ridiculously long.

After a while, Charlie had to say something. 'How much more can there be?'

'It's . . . never-ending,' said Flora.

'Like a waterfall in spring,' added Mohsen.

'That's a beautiful description, thank you, Mohsen,' said Wogan, still weeing.

'My pleasure,' said Mohsen.

'Can you PLEASE just finish?' said Charlie.

Finally – FINALLY – the wee finished. Mohsen's sandwich box was full to the brim.

Mohsen looked at it and shook his head. 'I don't know *what* I'm going to tell my mum.'

'OK,' said Wogan, 'I know we're still stuck in a lift and the police are probably about to come, and we are all going to get arrested, and the plan will have failed, and we'll all go to jail, and the only person to come to visit us will be Dylan just to laugh at us, but I'll tell you one thing: I feel a LOT better after that wee. Wow. SUCH a relief. Thanks, Moh. Say sorry to your mum for me.'

Wogan was right, thought Charlie. The police probably were on their way. The plan would fail. They'd all get arrested and it would be Charlie's fault. His parents would have to sell the house. He'd have to move. He'd lose his friends. And if he was in prison, there'd be no way to hide his changing.

And that was all it took.

'Guys! I'm changing!'

They all swung round to look at Charlie.

He could feel the electricity hitting him hard.

Flora's eyes widened. 'Try to stop it, Charlie!'

But it was all too much – the background

worry of the house, and the now-worry of being stuck in the lift. There was no stopping it this time. It was like a raging forest fire rampaging through him. He was going to change – and it was going to happen in this tiny lift.

'I can't. W-what . . .' Charlie managed to stammer. 'What happens if I change into something big?'

Flora, Wogan and Mohsen gulped and pushed themselves back against the sides of the lift. If Charlie changed into an elephant, for instance, they were all finished. They'd be squished completely.

They held their breath as they watched, terrified.

The electricity was tearing through Charlie now. He felt like he was being turned inside out.

His arms were shrinking.

So were his legs.

And so was the rest of him.

He wasn't growing bigger!

He was getting smaller!

If Charlie wasn't busy turning from a boy into an animal, he would have breathed a huge sigh of relief.

He was definitely getting smaller. And scalier.

His legs and arms had gone.

He was small now.

Very small.

He had . . . fins?

'Look!' said Mohsen. 'He's a goldfish!'

I'm a goldfish, thought Charlie. *Well, that's just* marvellous.[24] *Of all the useless animals to turn into. A* goldfish.

He lay on the floor of the lift, flapping slightly, his mouth opening and closing slowly.

Well, this is just fan-flipping-tastic.[25]

Wogan leaned over Charlie the goldfish. 'Can you hear us, Charlie?'

Charlie flapped his tail to say, *Yes, I can. I can hear you.*

Wogan stood back up. 'Is he OK?'

'What do you mean?' asked Flora.

---

[24] Charlie is being sarcastic here. Being sarcastic is when you say one thing but you actually mean the opposite. So Charlie actually means that it's really not in the least bit marvellous being a goldfish. That is actually a silly opinion because goldfish are, in fact, third on the Official List of Happiest Animals in the World. Second happiest are the tree-climbing goats of Morocco and the happiest animals in the world are actually dung beetles, because rolling balls of poo and then eating them actually makes them happy. The least happy animals in the world are humans. That's why you should try whenever you can to be as much like other animals as much as possible: swim like a dolphin, run like a cheetah, jump like a kangaroo, roll balls of poo around like a dung beetle. An interesting fact about dung beetles is that they are the only animals apart from humans that are known to navigate using the Milky Way, which is the galaxy we are in.

[25] He's being sarcastic again here.

'Well, he's a fish. And he's on the floor of a lift. No water. Can he breathe?'

Flora, Wogan and Mohsen looked at each other nervously.

'That's a good point,' said Mohsen.

I'm fine, Charlie flapped. *Really*.

'Look, his flapping is getting worse!' said Mohsen.

'Oh, my goodness!' Flora cried. 'You're right! He's struggling to breathe! Poor Charlie!'

I'm FINE, Charlie flapped. He felt a little dry, and a little short of breath, but he was mostly OK.

'Is there a chance,' Wogan said, looking stricken, 'that if we are stuck in here without water, Charlie could . . . die?'

Silence hit the lift, apart from the tiny sound of Charlie opening and closing his mouth, desperately trying to say 'Guys, don't worry, I'll be fine!'

'I had a goldfish once,' said Mohsen. 'He flipped himself out of his bowl when we were out shopping. When we got home he was lying on the floor. Dried-out. And dead.'

'OK,' said Flora. 'Does anybody have ANY water on them?'

Mohsen shook his head. 'Wogan drank it all when he arrived.'

'Gah!' said Flora, frustrated. 'Of course he did. That's why he needed a wee so badly. Oh! There must be something in here! If only we had a . . . container . . . full of liquid.' Her eyes flicked to the corner of the lift.

No, thought Charlie.

Flora was eyeing the box of yellow liquid that a couple of minutes ago had been shooting out of Wogan.

No, thought Charlie. *Anything but that!*

Wogan and Mohsen finally realized what Flora was thinking.

'You want to put Charlie in the sandwich box of Wogan's wee?' asked Mohsen in amazement.

No, no, no! flapped Charlie, panicking. *Noooo!*

'We don't have a choice!' said Flora. 'Look how much he's flapping! He can't breathe!'

I'm fine! Charlie flapped desperately. And then he stopped flapping to show just how fine he was.

'Oh, look!' cried Flora. 'He's stopped flapping! He's dying! Quickly! We need to do it now!'

Wogan kneeled down and very gently picked Charlie up by the tail, and carried him over to the sandwich box.

Charlie started flapping again in a panic.

No! Don't do it! DO NOT PUT ME IN THE WEE!

'Do it,' said Flora gravely.

NOOOOOOOOOOOO! flapped Charlie, suspended above the wee.

And then Wogan dropped him.

Charlie soared through the air for a second, and then landed in the single worst warm bath he had ever had.

It's impossible to describe Charlie's feelings as he swam around in his best friend's wee.

'He actually looks like he's enjoying himself in there,' said Wogan.

This was the most extremely wrong thing that anybody had ever said in the whole history of humans saying wrong things.

This, thought Charlie, trying to hold his breath, *is the ACTUAL, ACTUAL worst. Nothing will ever, ever, ever, EVER be worse than this.*

'You're right,' said Mohsen. 'He seems to be swimming around quite happily.'

This was the second most wrong thing that anybody had ever said in the whole history of humans saying wrong things.

When I get out of this, thought Charlie, *I'm going to —*

But no, Charlie realized. He had more urgent things to think about. And the number-one thing was getting out of this box. He had to change back. And that meant relaxing – no matter how hard it was to relax swimming around in Wogan's wee.

Charlie couldn't close his eyes because he didn't have any eyelids, and he couldn't breathe really deeply, because he was surrounded by wee, so he just had to concentrate on thinking happy, relaxing thoughts: finding out his brother was well again . . . going to Disneyland Paris two summers ago with his family . . . playing with his friends . . .

And then he felt, with the hugest sense of relief, electricity surging through his body again. Charlie felt like he was being squeezed through an infinitely coiling tube that went from one side of the universe and back again.

A moment later, Charlie the boy was back, standing in the corner of the lift, one foot in the sandwich box and drenched from head to toe in wee.

A look of wild, thunderous fury on Charlie's face dared anybody to say a word to him. They didn't.

'WHY,' shouted Charlie, 'WHY WOULD . . . WHY WOULD YOU *DO* THAT?'

Flora had the face of a nervous mouse. 'We just thought –'

'DON'T. JUST. DO. NOT. EVER.'

Flora, Wogan and Mohsen stood terrified and silent. The noise of Charlie's dripping clothes seemed to echo in the lift.

'NO ONE IS EVER – *EVER* – TO MENTION THIS AGAIN. DO YOU ALL UNDERSTAND?'

The three friends all nodded in terror.

'THIS NEVER HAPPENED, CORRECT?'

They nodded again.

And then, with a sudden whirr and a clunk, the lift started working again.

CHAPTER 10

'That's odd,' said Flora with a hint of concern in her voice. 'Why would the lift just start working again all by itself? Something's not right.'

No one had an answer to that mystery, but they were all very glad the lift *was* working again and that there was now something to distract Charlie from his wee-soaked hair and clothes.

A moment later, the lift pinged and the doors slid open.

Flora poked her head out of the lift and looked both ways. 'All clear. Which way, Wogan?'

Wogan squinted at his map. 'I'm not sure.

Charlie splashed some of my wee on the map, and it's all a bit blurry now. But I think it's left.'

'Well,' said Charlie, 'there's only one way to find out.'

Charlie strode out of the lift, and the others quickly followed. With each step Charlie took on the marble floor, his shoes squelched and squeaked.

'Charlie!' hissed Flora. 'Your shoes are very noisy!'

'There's not much I can do about that,' snapped Charlie. 'They appear to be soaked in wee FOR SOME REASON.'

Nobody had anything to say to that.

At the end of the long corridor there was a large grey door.

'I think this might be it,' said Wogan, squinting at the damp map.

He pushed the door and they all piled in.

The door led to a small platform, which

hung over a vast room. Inside the room were hundreds, possibly thousands, of chickens.

They stared silently at the four interlopers. Countless unblinking eyes glinted coldly. The friends stared back.

A few low, threatening clucks echoed around the chamber.

'I think,' whispered Wogan, 'this might be the wrong room.'

They edged backwards out of the room, never taking their eyes off the staring chickens for a second.

Wogan quietly shut the door behind them.

'We shall never talk of that room again,' said Mohsen, his face pale.

They all murmured in agreement, and then ran down the corridor opposite until they arrived at another door, a huge wooden one with a gleaming brass nameplate that said:

MR VAN DER GRUYNE
PRESIDENT
VAN DER GRUYNE INDUSTRIES

KNOCK THREE TIMES
DO NOT ENTER UNLESS YOU ARE
A VERY IMPORTANT PERSON

'This is it,' said Wogan. He lifted his fist up to the door and knocked slowly three times.

'Why are you knocking?' asked Flora.

'Because it says to!' replied Wogan, pointing at the nameplate. 'Flora, you really need to get your head in the game.'

Silence greeted the knock.

'I don't think there's anybody in there!' whispered Mohsen urgently. 'What do we do now?'

'We go in!' Flora said, and pulled the brass handle. The door opened silently.

Flora, Mohsen and Wogan padded quietly into the room, followed by Charlie, who squelched noisily into the room, each step leaving a yellow footprint on the thick cream carpet.

There was a huge mahogany desk in the centre of the room with a computer on it. The walls were lined with old leather-bound books.

There were no chairs in the room except the one behind the desk – clearly visitors to Mr Van der Gruyne's office were expected to stand. An antique globe, all wood and brass, stood in one corner. There was one thing missing, though. There was no safe.

'There's no safe,' said Mohsen, repeating what the narrator had just said.

Maybe there's a safe hidden somewhere, thought the narrator.

'Maybe there's a safe hidden somewhere,' said Flora, as if reading the thoughts of the narrator. *Get out of my head, Flora.*

The four started searching. About three seconds later, they stopped searching as there was nowhere else to look.

'That's it then. We're stuffed,' said Wogan. 'It's not here. Now what do we do, search every room in the building? That could take days.'

As Wogan spoke, he leaned one hand against

the globe. It immediately spun, and he slipped forward, his fingers jamming between the globe and the frame. At that moment Mohsen, Flora and Charlie all heard a tiny sound.

'What was that clicking noise?' asked Flora.

'I think that was my finger breaking,' whimpered Wogan.

'No, it wasn't that,' said Flora. 'It sounded like it came from behind these books.' Flora went over to the shelf and started pulling books off. 'Maybe there's something hidden here. A lever or something,' she continued.

'Hello!' called Wogan. 'My fingers are still stuck in the globe! Could one of you give me a hand here?'

'Look! Up there!' Mohsen pointed at a book on the top shelf, which stuck out further than the others. 'Maybe the globe triggered some sort of mechanism and pushed that book out. Come on, give me a hand up.'

'My fingers really are actually quite sore,' said Wogan, still attached to the globe.

Charlie rushed over to Mohsen, and gave him a leg-up.

Mohsen pulled the book free. 'There's a button behind it!'

'Well, press it!'

Mohsen pressed the button and immediately a whirring, vibrating thrum filled the room.

The globe suddenly started moving across the floor as if pulled by some unseen force.

Wogan yelped. 'It's got me, it's got me! It won't let me go!'

Charlie and Flora rushed over to Wogan and started pulling on his hand. After some serious tugging, he broke free, and all three fell backwards. The globe had stopped moving, but where it had been a trapdoor was now revealed. And there was something coming up through it.

It was a slowly rising platform, and on top of the platform was a great black metal box.

It was the safe.

'It's the safe!' said Mohsen, once again repeating exactly what the increasingly frustrated narrator had JUST said.

The four circled the safe, examining it. It looked heavy, and very old. There was a dial on it, and a solid slightly rusty iron handle. Charlie tried the handle. It was locked.

'I guess it was worth a go,' Charlie said with a rueful smile.

Mohsen rubbed his chin thoughtfully. 'OK, so we found it, but how do we open it?'

'Charlie, now's your time. We need you to change,' said Flora, putting a hand on his shoulder.

'Flora!' Charlie shouted, knocking the hand off his shoulder on to the floor. 'Seriously, that thing is just creepy. Please just stick it in the bin.'

'Flora's right, Charlie,' said Mohsen. 'We can't open the safe on our own. We need *animal* strength.'

Charlie swallowed. 'OK. I'll try.'

'Oh, you'll do more than try,' came a sudden voice. 'You *will* change. Or else.'

The friends swung round. Standing behind

them was the last person on earth they wanted
to see.

Dylan.

He fixed them with a grin dripping with
such malevolence it seemed to make the whole
room go darker.

'Fools! I've been following you the whole
time! You've been – Hang on, why does it smell
of wee in here?'

'Do NOT ask,' warned Wogan.

'Seriously. Don't,' agreed Mohsen.

Dylan saw the looks of fear on their faces, and sensibly heeded their warning. 'OK,' he continued. 'Anyway. So, as I was saying . . . I've been following you the whole time! And you have walked right into my trap. Welcome to my cobweb, spiders!'

'We're spiders?' asked Wogan. 'In a cobweb?

Isn't that a good thing?'

Dylan frowned. 'No! It's not! I'm a big spider! And you're smaller spiders. And I'm going to eat you!'

Mohsen turned to Wogan. 'He should have just called us flies. That would have made much more sense.'

'Yes, he's clutching at straws with the whole big-spider-eating-small-spiders thing.'

'Shut up!' screamed Dylan.

Wogan, Flora, Charlie and Mohsen's jaws all dropped.

'Dylan,' said Flora, steel in her voice. 'Now THAT was rude. There is no excuse for just telling someone to shut up. It's incredibly bad manners.'

Dylan looked shamefaced and mumbled 'sorry' to the floor.

'Apology accepted,' said Flora. 'Do carry on. What were you going to say anyway, Dylan?'

Dylan looked like he had quite lost his train of thought.

'Ermm . . . I've done "it's a trap" . . . then "cobweb and spiders" . . . Ah! Ah, yes! I know where I was. The big reveal! So, I've been watching you the whole time! Who do you think told the guards to leave the gate wide open? Who do you think turned off the alarm? And who do you think stopped the lift just for the pleasure of making you squirm? It was me! Me! And you've been my . . . my . . . puppets! Yes, puppets! Puppets works, doesn't it?'

Everybody nodded.

'Yup!'

'That actually works.'

'Good metaphor.'

'Thank you,' said Dylan with a proud smile. 'So here's what's going to happen next, losers. You're caught in my trap. And now, Charlie, you're going to change. Right here and right now. And I'm going to record it and use it to become famous. So start changing. Or else.'

Charlie puffed his chest up. 'Or else what?'

'Or else this.'

With a flourish Dylan produced a key from his pocket. He waggled it at Charlie, then swung round and locked the door, then pocketed the key again. From his other pocket he produced a mobile phone.

'Now,' he continued, 'you're all locked in here. So, Charlie McGuffin, you either change or I call the police and tell them how I caught you in my dad's office trying to open his safe. What's the punishment for attempted burglary? Definitely jail. And all your friends will be arrested too, McGuffin. They'll probably go to jail as well. So – it's your choice. You either change into something or I call the police and drop you and your friends into more trouble than you ever dreamed of. So, what's it to be?'

'Don't listen to him, Charlie,' said Flora. 'We don't care. We're doing the right thing, and I'm proud. Let him call the police.'

'That's right!' said Wogan. 'Don't change! That'll wipe the smug face off his face.'

'Yeah,' said Mohsen. 'Bog off, Dylan, you big bargle-faced snarf-wangler.'

Everybody gasped. And rightfully so,

because that was quite some brutal insulting from Mohsen.

'Thanks, guys,' said Charlie, turning to his friends. 'But Dylan already knows what I'm going to choose. I can't get you guys in trouble.'

'But we don't care!' said Wogan.

'Honestly, Charlie!' said Flora. 'You'd do it for us!'

'I would, that's right. And every one of you, if you were in my position, would do what I'm about to do so the others don't get into trouble. That's why I'm going to do it. I'm going to change.'

Mohsen gasped. 'No, Charlie,' he said. 'Please don't!'

'It's too late. Stand back, guys. Here I go.'

'OK,' said Dylan, raising his phone. 'I'm recording. Off you go, freak-boy.'

'You don't have to do this, Charlie!' cried Flora.

'I do, Flora. I do.' Charlie gave Flora the slightest wink to try to show he wasn't bothered.

But he was.

This was it. Not only had Dylan won, but his own plan had failed. They had come so close to getting back his dad's gold, but he had messed it up. He was useless. His parents were going to lose their house and Charlie was going to lose his friends. And who knew what would happen to him when Dylan revealed the video to the world.

Everything had gone wrong.

But at least he could get one thing right and stop his friends from getting into trouble.

Charlie closed his eyes.

All his fears flooded into him.

All the misery and the anguish and the anxiety began to worm in his stomach, transforming into an electrical fire that tore through his brain, every breath he took crackling with static.

Something, though, suddenly felt different.

This time, the fire in him felt completely out of control.

He was being overwhelmed by the power surging through him, almost as if all the energy in the universe was tearing his very atoms apart.

Charlie looked at Flora, eyes filled with panic, and was able to utter a single desperate word.

'Run!'

CHAPTER 11

It wasn't the word 'Run!' that frightened Flora, or the way Charlie had said it – it was the look of real terror in Charlie's eyes.

'Come on!' she cried. 'We have to go! NOW!'

She ran to the door and pulled on the handle, but it was still locked.

'Dylan! Unlock the door,' she shouted.

'Not a chance!' said Dylan, pointing his phone straight at Charlie.

'Dylan!'

'No! No way am I missing this!'

Charlie was desperately battling to slow his change down to give his friends time to escape. He was doing everything he could, trying to breathe slowly and remembering all the good things in his life. But as soon as he thought of any happy thoughts they blew away from him like the last leaves of autumn. The storm inside him was raging.

'Dylan, if you don't open this door we could all get very badly hurt! Please,' Flora begged.

'Yeah, nice try,' Dylan replied.

Flora strode right up to Dylan and went nose to nose with him. She started speaking very quietly. 'Dylan. If you don't open this door immediately, I will be forced to punch you. And then kick you. I don't want to, but I will. And if you have any doubts that I'll do it, look into my eyes. Look deep into my eyes. Can you see it? That's right. That's your doom you see there, Dylan Van der Gruyne.

NOW. OPEN. THIS. DOOR.'

Dylan swallowed nervously. 'Fine!' He

swung round and unlocked the door.

Flora, Mohsen and Wogan charged through and started running down the corridor. But Flora stopped when she realized they weren't being followed.

Dylan was still recording Charlie.

Charlie's face was creased with concentration.

'Dylan! You need to come with us!' shouted Flora. 'You're in terrible danger!'

Dylan looked from Charlie to Flora and back to Charlie again.

'GAH, OK!' he cried, and he started running towards Flora.

And the second they escaped the room, the fire in Charlie finally exploded. He felt himself torn apart, growing, every part of him stretching.

He was filling the room.

His expanding body smashed through the wall of the office, knocking it down like paper.

He could just make out the small figures of his friends at the end of the corridor, running in terror. As he grew and grew, crushing the desk and computer under him, he saw them turn the corner and start down the stairs.

Charlie was long now, as long as the corridor, but he was still growing. He smashed through the walls of the corridor, expanding into the chamber of chickens, scattering poultry in a storm of outraged clucking. He tried his hardest to slow his growth down, desperately clinging on to distant happy memories, but the fear that he might crush his friends turned those happy thoughts to ice.

Charlie didn't need a mirror to tell him what he was turning into.

There was only one thing it could be.

Only one thing *that* enormous.

He was a whale.[26]

He felt his back scraping the ceiling and the floor below him buckling under his huge weight. He could feel a great tail at the end of his body, swishing slightly, some instinct driving it to swim,

---

[26] The blue whale is not just the biggest creature in the world, it's the biggest creature that EVER EXISTED. Bigger than any dinosaur. It's not the biggest creature in the universe, though. As I'm sure you all know, the biggest creature in the universe is the lesser spotted pan-galactic brainglobe, which eats planets for breakfast and black holes for dinner. Luckily for us the brainglobe lives in the far left-hand corner of the universe, and doesn't come near our part of the universe.

Yet.

but with each swish it knocked into the wall, causing dust and debris to fall on to Charlie's head.

Charlie tried to stay as still as possible and focus on changing back to Charlie. A broken silence settled in the building. Only the sounds of plaster crumbling from the ceiling and the

distant pattering of his friends' footsteps interrupted the quiet. And then there was a vast creak that Charlie felt underneath the whole length of his huge body. It could only mean one thing.

Suddenly the floor beneath Charlie gave

up. It could no longer take his weight. Charlie smashed through the collapsing floor and into the level below. He hurtled down, and then smashed through the floor of that level too, taking printers, pot plants and desks with him.

His speed and weight took him straight through the next level too, and the one after that. Finally he crash-landed in the basement room, on a bed of crushed computer equipment – the servers that kept all of Van der Gruyne Industries' information, the same computers they had seen when they first entered the building, and which were now completely destroyed.

He lay there, breathing heavily through the blowhole at the top of his head. A few chickens clucked and pecked around him, and a handful of loose feathers floated in the dusty air. He was relieved to be still again, no longer crashing through ceilings and floors, but he was desperately worried for his friends. Had they made it out safely? Or had they been horribly caught up in the destruction caused by a massive whale collapsing through the building?

Everything I do just makes things worse for my friends, Charlie thought, his heart aching with misery. Because HE was in trouble, his friends had got themselves into this horribly dangerous adventure. Charlie just prayed they had all escaped in time – even Dylan.

Whatever had happened, Charlie knew he didn't deserve friends like Flora, Mohsen and Wogan. They were too good for him, and they'd be a lot safer and happier if he just moved away from them anyway.

Charlie's vast black eyes saw the destruction around him – the destruction of the building and the destruction of his dreams, and he let out a great sigh through his blowhole, and the sigh felt like an ending.

Without realizing quite what he was doing, Charlie started to sing. A slow, mournful song that seemed to contain all the sadness in the world. It was the music of melting snow and forgotten myths, and cold empty universes collapsing in on themselves, and with each melancholy note he sang Charlie began to forget who he was. He was the whale, and Charlie was no more. The low notes reverberated and shook the building, the long high notes were a lament to –

'Would you cut that racket out? I can't hear myself think!'

Charlie's huge heart practically leaped out of his body. That voice! He remembered! It was Wogan! He was safe! Charlie couldn't turn but he could hear feet crunching through the debris on the floor.

'Seriously! It's giving me a headache,' continued Wogan. 'I bet they can hear it from miles away.'

'Well, *I* thought it was rather lovely actually.'

That was Flora's voice, and Charlie didn't think he had ever heard a more beautiful sound in his life, hearing her and knowing she was safe too.

'Not sure Dylan would agree. That noise had him running out of the building with his fingers in his ears.' And that was it. That was Mohsen's voice. All his friends were safe, and nothing else mattered to Charlie. 'Actually,' Mohsen continued, 'whales usually only sing when they are deep in the water. We're very lucky to hear it.'

Charlie felt a soft hand on his flank.

'And to see him!' Charlie heard Flora say. 'Just look at him! He's extraordinary.'

Flora walked next to Charlie, trailing her hand along his body until she arrived at his eye.

She smiled. 'Hello there, you.'

Charlie thought he would burst with happiness.

'It's time for you to change back to Charlie.'

She's right, thought Charlie. It was time. But then he remembered how much danger he had put his friends in, and how much trouble they would definitely now be in. All because of him.

And he found he didn't want to change back. He just wanted to lie there.

'Come on, Charlie,' said Mohsen. 'Dylan's getting away. We need to catch him and get his phone, in case he recorded anything!'

Charlie let out a small huff from his blowhole in reply.

'Charlie,' said Flora, looking sternly into his eye. 'We need you to come back. The four of us stick together whatever, so you have to come back to us.'

With a great effort Charlie closed his eyelid so he could blank out the sight of Flora. It was too painful to see her, knowing how much trouble he had got them in. How he had nearly killed them all.

'Now look here, Charlie McGuffin!' shouted Flora, pulling up the great flap of Charlie's eyelid so he had to look at her. 'You need to snap out of this. You may be a whale but I can still tell when you are feeling sorry for yourself, with all that huffing and puffing out of your blowhole! It's time you realized that me, Wogan and Mohsen are our own people and able to make our own decisions! We decided to help you! You didn't make us. So this isn't all your fault. We are a team, and we stick together, and that is what friends are for.'

Somewhere deep down in the hidden depths of Whale-Charlie's mind a light flickered in the darkness. The light felt something like happiness.

Wogan crunched up to Charlie's eye, and started shouting as well. 'And another thing: you're a great big whale and you're on dry land and you'll die without water. And I'm sorry to say there's not a sandwich box full of wee to save you this time. I'd have to fill an Olympic-sized swimming pool and that would take ages. And I don't even need a wee right now.'

Mohsen walked up to Charlie's head. 'I actually do need a wee,' he said, a look of great seriousness on his face. 'Maybe if we all weed in something together, we could . . .'

Flora gave Mohsen a withering stare.

'I just thought . . . you know . . .' he continued nervously. 'Like you said . . . we should all stick together . . .'

Wogan nodded. 'Yes! If we all wee together, then maybe –'

Flora had had enough. 'That is the worst idea you two have *ever* come up with! You want to stick Charlie in your wee AGAIN?! What even do you think you are going to wee into? Do you happen to have an Olympic-sized swimming pool handy? And if you did, do you have ANY idea how long it would take to fill it with wee?[27] No! Exactly! You are the biggest pair of –'

And as he watched his friends arguing over Olympic-sized swimming pools of wee Charlie felt happiness flood through him. He didn't deserve such good friends, but he was very lucky to have them. And just like that, Charlie began to change.

He shrank and shrank until he was a normal boy again.

[27] Interesting question, Flora. Let's do the maths! An average Olympic-sized swimming pool needs about three million litres of water (or wee) to be filled. An average child does just over half a litre of wee a day. That means if Flora, Mohsen and Wogan did all their wees in an Olympic-sized swimming pool every single day, it would take about two million days – or to put it another way, nearly 5,500 years – to fill the pool! So that goes to show it was indeed one of the worst plans Mohsen and Wogan had ever concocted.

A normal boy, surrounded by his three best friends, in a building he had accidentally just half destroyed.

He stood up and dusted himself down, a wide smile on his face. 'Hi, guys,' Charlie said, grinning. 'I have to say I'm delighted that you didn't have a swimming pool full of wee as –'

Charlie stopped talking as soon as he saw it.

There in the corner of the room.

The safe from Mr Van der Gruyne's office. It must have come tumbling all the way down with Charlie.

And, unbelievably, Charlie could see the door was open a crack. It must have broken open in the collapse. The friends all saw where Charlie was looking.

'Go on, Charlie,' said Mohsen. 'Go and look in it.'

Charlie was frozen to the spot, though, not daring to believe what he was seeing – that by some extraordinary accident the safe with the stolen gold in was actually now open – not daring to dream that he might have just saved his parents.

Finally Charlie crunched over to the safe, hopping over chickens, nerves jangling. He knelt down, dragged open the huge door and looked inside.

CHAPTER 12

Charlie looked at his friends, aghast. 'It's empty,' he said flatly.

'Empty?' asked Wogan.

Charlie nodded.

'Like COMPLETELY empty?'

Charlie nodded again.

Wogan stormed over to the safe, and popped his head inside.

'It's empty,' he said, his head still in the safe.

'Like COMPLETELY empty?' asked Mohsen.

Wogan nodded, but nobody saw because his head was still in the safe.

'Well, that's it,' said Charlie. 'I'm finished. Done for. No gold means my parents have to sell the house and we have to move into Aunt Brenda's. This is goodbye, guys.'

Silence fell on the four friends like fog at night.

Charlie sat on the floor, head in hands. He felt utterly defeated.

'And just look at this place,' he added. 'All this mess. For nothing.'

Flora, Wogan and Mohsen, looked around in silence.

Charlie fell back and groaned. 'I just want to change into a slug or something and slime off under a rock and completely forget that I'm Charlie.'

'Dylan,' said Flora abruptly.

The others looked at her.

'What about him?' Wogan said.

'He must know where the gold is hidden.'

'Yeah, probably,' Wogan said. 'But he'll never tell us.'

Flora thumped her palm. 'We'll make him!'

'But he's gone! He ran out of the building.'

'We can catch him! Or Charlie can at least. He just needs to change into something fast.'

Charlie looked up. Despite everything, a sliver of hope gleamed in his eyes. 'I guess it might be worth a try . . .'

'That's the spirit! Come on!'

The four friends started running, and then sprang up the half-destroyed stairs. A moment later they were standing outside the gate of Van der Gruyne Industries, scanning for Dylan.

'There!' shouted Flora. 'At the end of the street!'

In the distance was a small figure – and it was unmistakably Dylan.

'Now quick, Charlie! Change!' Flora urged. 'Think of something fast! A cheetah would be perfect. When you change, keep the image of a cheetah in your mind!'

His friends edged backwards, the whale incident still pretty fresh in their minds because:

1. It had only happened a few minutes ago.
2. Their best friend had just turned into an enormous whale and back again, and

when you see your friend turn into an actual whale and back again, it tends to stay quite fresh in your mind.

Charlie closed his eyes. It was easy to change this time. He just remembered how he'd felt just a few moments ago by the empty safe. The electricity tore straight through him. He could feel his body changing almost immediately. And as he changed he tried to keep a picture of a cheetah in the front of his mind.

He was growing fur. That was a good sign.

He felt that squeezing sensation that made him feel like he was being turned inside out. Still he pictured the cheetah sprinting majestically across the savannah.

He could tell he now had four legs. Another good sign.

The change was finishing. He was nearly the complete animal.

He was growing claws. Fur, four long legs, claws? Had he done it? Had he finally discovered how to choose which animal to change into?

Charlie started running after Dylan as fast as he could. He felt strong and powerful as he pushed his new body to unimaginable speed . . .

'Charlie.'

As he ran, Charlie turned his head towards Flora. He didn't seem to have moved very far from his friends considering he had been running as fast as he could. In fact, he seemed to have moved less than half a metre from where he had started.

'Charlie,' repeated Flora. 'You're a sloth, Charlie.'

I'm a what?

Charlie's jaw dropped. Very slowly.

A sloth? Of all the bloomin' useless animals to turn into now, Charlie thought slowly. *Well, never mind – this sloth is going to have to run faster than any sloth has ever run before if Dylan isn't going to get away!*

Charlie picked up his speed, his legs pumping as hard as possible, wind whistling in his fur, the world a blur.

'Oh dear,' Flora said as she walked slowly to stand by Charlie's side. 'A sloth!'

Charlie felt slightly miffed that despite his furious pace, Flora seemed able to match his speed by plodding slowly next to him.

'Oh, Charlie, a sloth!' Flora said, a tinkle of laughter in her voice.

What's so funny about that? thought Charlie.

'Yeah, hurry up, Charlie!' said Mohsen. 'If you keep up that pace, we should be able to catch Dylan some time next month!'

Wogan, Flora and Mohsen all burst out laughing.

Charlie finally stopped running and noticed to his surprise that this hardly changed his

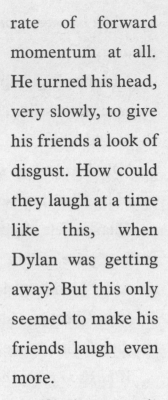

rate of forward momentum at all. He turned his head, very slowly, to give his friends a look of disgust. How could they laugh at a time like this, when Dylan was getting away? But this only seemed to make his friends laugh even more.

'Slothman is here to save the day!' Wogan said, doubling over with laughter, Flora and Mohsen roaring next to him.

And as Charlie watched his friends crying with laughter he had to admit there was a funny side to it. And so Charlie started chortling to himself, an odd sloth-snuffle of a chortle, which made him laugh even more. And as he laughed and laughed at the ludicrousness of needing to be the fastest animal on earth and changing into a sloth, Charlie changed back to Charlie, the normal-ish boy.

And then, even though Dylan was long gone and Charlie's plan was in tatters, all four friends clung to each other, tears of laughter streaming down their faces.

***

Once the laughter had eventually died down, though, it was a sombre walk home. Despite their best efforts, it had, in the end, all gone wrong. The friends said a sad goodbye as Charlie turned the corner into his street and trudged back alone to a quiet house.

SmoothMove was in his bedroom, his father had his head buried in papers, worry etched on his face, and his mother was tapping away with great concentration on her laptop, a concerned look on her face to match her husband's. There was an air of gloom that hung in the air like a thick gas, choking life from the house,[28] despite the Christmas carols that were playing on the radio in the empty kitchen.

Charlie sat in his room for hours tinkering with Lego and Meccano, until his belly rumbling told him it was teatime. He flumped downstairs to ask what they were having. Without even looking up from his papers, his dad muttered at Charlie to make himself some beans on toast.

[28] Rather like the leftover skunk pong that still permeated the place.

As Charlie stirred the beans in the pan, tears sprang into his eyes. He couldn't help it. As much as he tried to stop, the burning in his eyes and throat became worse. Fat teardrops finally dripped into the beans, and Charlie tried to choke back a sob in case his parents heard.

And to make matters even worse Charlie could feel himself changing, that familiar fire rushing through him. *Please*, Charlie thought miserably. *Not now. Just not now.*

Charlie's dad's phone suddenly started ringing on the kitchen table. Charlie swung back to the beans, hiding his tear-stained face as his dad came in to find it, desperately trying to slow his breathing down.

'Mm,' his dad said, answering the phone.

'What?' his dad continued. 'A what? Earthquake? At Van der Gruyne Industries? Don't be daft. It what? It WHAT? Give over. You can't be serious.'

His dad paused, listening, and Charlie could hear a tiny excited voice on the other end of the phone.

'What? ALL of it?' his dad continued. 'I don't believe it.'

There was an animated tone growing in his father's voice, one that Charlie hadn't heard in a long time. He hardly dared breathe as he tried to work out what was going on.

'All the computers were destroyed and

they've lost everything? Including our code?
You're sure? You're ABSOLUTELY certain?
But . . . but . . . that means we're saved! That's
absolutely extraordinary.'

Charlie plucked up the courage to turn
round. On his father's face was something
remarkable: a smile. A beaming smile. And that
smile immediately put out the terrible fire
burning inside Charlie.

'I don't believe it,' Charlie's dad said, shaking

his head. 'I just don't believe it. Talk about divine justice! A proper act of God! Good grief. Oh yes, definitely a bottle of bubbly. See you tomorrow!'

And with that Charlie's dad ended the call.

'Quick, everyone, get in here!' he called in breathless excitement.

As SmoothMove and Mum made their way in, Charlie's dad turned on his laptop and opened the local news website.

He pointed at the headline, spluttering, unable to get out any more words.

FREAK EARTHQUAKE DESTROYS BUILDING

'What?' Charlie's mum looked confused.

'Just . . . look,' replied his dad.

His mum started reading aloud from the website.

'A localized earthquake has partially destroyed the headquarters of Van der Gruyne

Industries. The surrounding area seems to be untouched, but reports indicate the inside of the building has been left in ruins. A spokesman for the company has said their entire computer system has been destroyed and the company will be out of action for months. Unfortunately all the CCTV cameras were also destroyed in the incident so we have no footage to show you. Happily there are no reports of any injuries, although several chickens who seem to have been roosting in the building are being treated for shock.'

The website included a video interview with Mr Van der Gruyne himself, his hair messy, ash all over his face. He was crying.

'It's not fair!' Mr Van der Gruyne wailed. 'Everything's destroyed! It's all gone! All my hard honest work up in smoke! I want my mummy!'

'Well, I never,' Charlie's mum said, laughing.

'And the truly extraordinary thing is,' his dad continued, 'because they lost all their server computers, that means they've also lost the code they stole from us!'

Charlie's mum whooped with delight and hugged his dad, giving him a huge kiss on his glowing cheek.

Charlie gasped. 'They lost the gold?'

'Gold?' his dad said, looking baffled. 'What are you talking about? What gold?'

'When we were out in town for SmoothMove's birthday, you told me that Mr Van der Gruyne stole gold from us, and you just said they lost it in the earthquake!'

'No, I didn't!' said his dad. 'I said code! They stole *code* from us, Charlie, not gold! You must have misheard! Code and gold – I suppose they sound similar. But no! They stole CODE from us. The computer code McGuffin & Sons has been developing for the last five years. With that code Van der Gruyne Industries were going to steal our biggest customer and leave us bankrupt. But now their computers have been destroyed, our company is safe! We don't have to move!'

Charlie's mum jumped forward and hugged her husband again.

SmoothMove gave Charlie a beaming smile. 'Looks like we aren't going to have to share a room at Aunt Brenda's after all.' He ruffled Charlie's hair and walked back upstairs.

Charlie stood there, open-mouthed. It had worked.

Somehow, some way, their plan had worked.

There'd never been any gold, but he had accidentally saved McGuffin & Sons. With a little help from his friends anyway.

OK, some people might say that a lot of it had been down to sheer blind luck. But no – not today.

Today, Charlie really *was* a superhero.

★★★

'I can't believe it,' said Flora, eyes wide in shock.

'Nor can I,' said Mohsen, eyes even wider in shock.

'Me neither,' said Wogan, eyes narrow with shock, because sometimes Wogan liked to do things differently.

Basically there had been a lot of wide-eyed shock and a small amount of narrow-eyed shock since Charlie had started recounting what he had found out on Saturday evening.

It was the last week of term. Excitement ran through the school and everybody was wearing Christmas jumpers. The friends were standing in the playground at lunch break. It was cold, and their breaths were little cloud explosions. The sky above them was deep grey, heavy with the possibility of snow. Wogan was wearing a woollen hat with a unicorn horn – an early Christmas present from Daisy. In the corner of the playground Miss Fyre and Mr Wind were standing next to each other in a very, very close huddle, presumably just trying to keep each other warm.

'I can't believe the plan actually worked,' said Flora, *still* shaking her head.

'Oh, Flora! Your plans always work – you should know that by now,' said Wogan.

'Gold! Code!' said Mohsen. 'Most people

would say you were a total wally for getting that wrong, Charlie, but I think they are very similar-sounding and it is an understandable mistake.'

'That's right, Mohsen,' said Wogan. 'For instance, I definitely think Charlie is a total wally for getting that wrong.'

Charlie grinned. 'Thanks for that, Wogan!'

'Hey, all's well that ends well!' said Flora.

Charlie had to agree. The for-sale sign in the garden had come down that morning and an air of happiness had returned to the house just in time for Christmas. But there was one question that still bothered Charlie, and the boy who could answer it was standing by the climbing frame trying to look menacing.

Charlie wandered over, trying his best to look nonchalant. 'Hello, Dylan,' he said.

'McGuffin. I might have guessed it was you.'

'Well, you didn't guess. You just watched me walk up to you.'

'What do you want, McGuffin?' sneered Dylan.

'I . . . I want answers.'

'Ha! We all want answers! What is the meaning of life? Why are you such a loathsome goody two-shoes? Why do I want to talk to girls AND not talk to them at the same time? So many questions, so few answers. Yet you expect answers from me.'

'Dylan, you could have told on us. You could have got all my friends in *serious* trouble. You could have told your dad about us breaking in to the office and destroying everything and yet you didn't. Why?'

'Are you really that stupid, McGuffin, or are you just pretending?' Dylan said. 'Can you imagine how that conversation would go? "Dad, Dad, you know you thought that your office got destroyed by an earthquake? Well, actually it was an idiot boy at my school who broke in and changed into a whale, destroyed everything and then changed back into a boy again." "Oh, really, Dylan? That sounds like a perfectly reasonable explanation and you haven't lost it at all. Here, have some extra pocket money for bringing this important and totally believable news to me." Yeah right. I'd be packed off to some School for Strange and Dangerous Children before you could say "Charlie McGuffin is a freak of nature."'

Charlie was beginning to think that a School for Strange and Dangerous Children might not be such a bad place for Dylan.

'But you were recording me. You could have shown them the recording. Unless . . .'

Charlie left the sentence hanging in the freezing air between them.

Dylan reached in his pocket and pulled out his phone. He turned it towards Charlie and started playing a video. It was grainy, wobbly footage of Charlie in Dylan's dad's office. Charlie was about to change. He could hear shouting in the background. And then, just as Charlie was about to change, just as he was about to start growing and expanding, the camera suddenly jerked and all he could see was upside-down footage of Dylan running down the corridor. And then the video stopped.

'But you could have shown that to your dad,' Charlie said. 'Or the police. It might have been enough to get them to investigate.'

Dylan sneered. 'And I still might do that. To tell you the truth, though, Charlie, you're the only thing that interests me in this tedious school. In short, I enjoy our little dance, McGuffin, and I'd like it to continue just that bit longer. I feel we have one more contest in us. A final battle of minds and wit and strength. Then we shall see who the final victor is. Until next time, Charles McGuffin.'

Dylan nodded, turned and walked off, nose in the air.

That boy, thought Charlie, *is absolutely bonkers.*

A single feathery snowflake drifted down and landed on Charlie's scarf. He lifted his head back and looked into the sky. More snow was to come.

And more danger . . .

Puffin Books

80 Strand

London

Dear Valued Reader,

Once again, we have reached the end of a book
by Sam Copeland, and found ourselves in an
awkward situation.

Despite the cover showing Charlie turning
into a T-Rex, there are clearly no dinosaurs in
this book.

First, you were cheated out of chickens,
and now dinosaurs.

As the publisher, we humbly apologize.

Although it's totally not our fault. It's Sam
Copeland's fault.

We hate him. He's a liar and he smells
weird – a bit like a cross between burnt toenail
clippings and frog poo.

Furthermore, his decision to pretend to put dinosaurs into this story merely as a greedy scheme to sell more copies to dinosaur-loving children is entirely deplorable. Please know that we, your beloved publisher, would NEVER be so cold, calculating and ruthless as to try to entice children into reading a book in this way.

Yours faithfully,

The Publisher

Dear Reader,

They totally would.

Sam Copeland

Dear Reader,

No, we wouldn't.

The Publisher

Dear Reader,

Yes, they would.

Sam Copeland

Dear Sam Copeland,

You'll be hearing from our lawyers.

The Publisher

Dear Publisher,

OOOOOOH I'M SOOOOO SCARED!

Sam Copeland

Dear Valued Readers,

Following a letter from the lawyers of Puffin Books, I have been instructed to make the following statement:

I am really very sorry for being a big horrible liar and making false accusations about my lovely publisher, who really are the best publisher in the world. Also, I smell of burnt toenail clippings and frog poo.

Yours faithfully,

Sam Copeland

Read on for
a sneak peek
of Charlie's
next adventure!

CHAPTER 1

Charlie McGuffin was late again.

And he really couldn't be late this time or he was a dead man.

Charlie had eighteen minutes to get to school if he didn't want to miss the coach, which was due to leave at precisely 9 a.m. to take his whole year to the zoo. Miss Fyre, the headmistress, had given them all a warning in assembly the day before: anyone who missed the bus would spend the whole day scrubbing the teachers' toilets with the caretaker, Mr O'Dere.

Charlie hoovered up his cornflakes,[1] flung

---

[1] He'd spilled them all over the floor.

on his coat and jumped into his shoes,[2] trying to ignore the sound of his parents arguing *again*. He flew out of the door,[3] hopped onto his trusty bike and started pedalling. That was when disaster struck.

His front wheel immediately started making an odd clicking noise and began to deflate. Charlie groaned. He *couldn't* have a puncture.

---

[2] This was why he was late – jumping into your shoes is actually very difficult and took him twenty-seven attempts.

[3] He hadn't really, he had just run. Ordinarily that wouldn't need to be pointed out, but because this is a book about a boy who can change into animals, I thought I should probably clarify. Don't worry, it's always very clear when Charlie's turning into an animal. It's not like he wakes up one morning and – BANG! – he's a gigantic insect and you're left wondering how on earth that happened. That would be terrible storytelling.

But a puncture it was. Dug deep into the tyre were four drawing pins. *Four?* How had *that* happened? Charlie looked down at the pavement and saw at least twenty more pins scattered all over the ground.

Somebody must have accidentally dropped a box and not picked them up, Charlie thought, without a hint of suspicion, which he really should have had, considering this is the start of the book and suspicious goings-on always happen at the start of books.

Well, that's just really bad luck, Charlie thought. *No one would put drawing pins on the pavement outside my house on purpose.*

Anyway, there was nothing he could do about it now. He was definitely going to be late and miss the school trip. Unless . . .

Unless . . .

Unless I change into an animal, Charlie thought. Then he might JUST have the time to fly to school or run there super-fast, change back without being seen AND catch the coach.

Charlie had been changing into animals for several months now, and had learned how to do it whenever he wanted. It was choosing *which* animal that he hadn't quite mastered . . . No matter what he did, it still seemed almost completely random.

Even so, changing was his only chance. It was a risk he had to take.

Charlie dumped his bike underneath a bush in his front garden, and glanced around to make sure there was nobody watching.

It looked like the coast was clear.

Charlie closed his eyes and balled his fists, allowing stress to flow into his body. He thought about the rumble of his parents' arguments, which seemed to be non-stop these days. The sound of their raised voices and slammed doors made Charlie feel like his lungs were too tight and his stomach had been dropped in icy water. He remembered running upstairs to his bedroom and finding the Great Catsby lying on his bed, out of his box in the kitchen for once, and burying his face in the cat's fur, sobbing.

Charlie recognized the feeling of electricity rippling through his body almost immediately.

He was changing, and changing fast.

Charlie tried imagining the quickest animal he could think of: a great, soaring bird sprang into his brain, a golden eagle with huge wings, designed for maximum speed.

He kept the picture in his mind as the electricity built and built, ripping apart every atom in his body and rebuilding them. He could sense himself shrinking and feel wings sprouting out of his back. But then, to Charlie's dismay, he continued shrinking. Smaller than a golden eagle . . .

Way smaller . . .

Maybe I'm going to be a pigeon again, Charlie thought with a groan. *PLEASE not a pigeon. ANYTHING but that!*

No, he realized with relief. *I'm even smaller than a pigeon.*

A sparrow?

No, smaller than a sparrow. And anyway, he wasn't growing feathers.

He *had* grown four new legs, some bristly hair and *three*

new eyes on his forehead, but no feathers. And his two original eyes had split into thousands of tiny eyes, *and* he'd grown antennae out of his head. Charlie was pretty sure no bird looked THAT freaky. He rubbed his two front legs together and buzzed a pair of fragile, transparent wings.

He was tiny now. The size of a –

Charlie was a *fly*.

Ah well, thought Charlie. *It could be worse.* He could still whizz to school super-fast, and while an eagle over the playground would have probably drawn a bit of attention, nobody would notice a boring old house fly, so Charlie reckoned he was pretty safe.

As long as he kept focused and didn't forget who he *really* was, that is. Because, as Charlie had discovered, becoming an animal sometimes made him start to forget that he was actually a human. And that meant trouble . . .

Charlie's antennae twitched, and a sudden

shiver of nervousness shot through his body. It felt like his body had some sort of tingling fly sixth sense, on high alert to any danger.

With a final rub of his front legs, Charlie buzzed his wings and zipped into the air. He had a curious feeling he was being watched but, despite his many eyes, he couldn't see anybody, so he put it to the back of his tiny fly-mind and started off in the direction of school.

Charlie zoomed happily along, his wings whirring so fast they were a blur. He would never get bored of the feeling of flying – he felt so free, so agile. Plus, his new fly-vision gave him an incredible 360-degree view of the world. It was strange to be flying forward but able to see behind him at the same time. The people and cars below seemed to be moving incredibly slowly. Compared to Charlie, they were crawling in slow-motion. He could see a boy cycling below him who looked like he was peddling through water.

Suddenly, Charlie's antennae twitched again.

He could smell something *delicious*.

Well, Charlie thought, *I did miss out on my cornflakes. And I'm making such good progress, I reckon I've got time for a quick snack* . . .

Charlie the fly followed the irresistible smell drifting through the air, zig-zagging closer and closer.

Finally, he spotted the source.

There, on the ground.

A scrumptious, exquisite, delicious-looking mound of brown steaming poo.

Yum, thought Charlie.